CHAPTER ONE

FREE GIFT

'Bud' Lockhart, hydraulic engineer, listened approvingly as Terence Oden, leader of the Dry River ranchers addressed them. Lockhart sat in the front row of desks in the little schoolhouse which was being used for the meeting.

Oden, a lean, somber Texan with crisp graying hair and a close-clipped, wiry black mustache, had a succinct way of putting things. He accented his points by slamming a brown, big-knuckled fist into the palm of the other hand.

'Shore we need a dam,' Oden declared, his steady eyes seeming to fix each individual in the audience. 'If one of you boys has said it once, we've all said it a thousand times. But it's talk, talk, talk. For years we've talked about a dam to carry us through the seasonal droughts, but we never done anything about it.' His clenched fist rose high. 'This time it's different!' he shouted. 'We're goin' to have a dam!'

Smack went the fist, and Lockhart smiled as the cowmen cheered. The power of words was tremendous. They could stir men to greater deeds than the ordinary erection of an

1

artificial barrier to prevent a small stream from dissipating its much needed waters. Words could start wars, bring peace, whip men into dying for a cause.

Lockhart suddenly realized that he was smiling at Lily Oden, Terence's daughter, who was sitting in the front row not far from him. He had met her at Oden's Dot O, which lay north of the Texas settlement. Since then interest in life had quickened for him, and the future had taken on a roseate hue. He thought that the job of constructing Dry River Dam should prove to be an extraordinarily pleasant one. He was young enough to feel proud of his skill and the fact that he would loom as an important figure in Lily's eyes.

Inclined to philosophize, he decided that other things than words also had power. Say, for instance, shining dark hair, roses blooming in smooth young cheeks, smiling blue eyes with long lashes—all belonging to a slim young girl in a starched white dress, with a ribbon bow at her throat. The power a girl like that had was one which made a young engineer hungry for success, made him forget the oppressive heat of this early evening, and the smell of oiled leather, dusty riding clothes, and warm humanity.

Oden's words became just a drone in the background as Bud Lockhart contemplated Lily Oden.

'—and so we worked at it quiet-like, ladies

2

F.L

DAZ.

HELL IN PARADISE

HELL IN PARADISE

Jackson Cole

Chivers Press • **G.K. Hall & Co.**
Bath, England   **Waterville, Maine USA**

This Large Print edition is published by Chivers Press, England, and by G.K. Hall & Co., USA.

Published in 2001 in the U.K. by arrangement with the author c/o Golden West Literary Agency.

Published in 2001 in the U.S. by arrangement with Golden West Literary Agency.

U.K. Hardcover   ISBN 0-7540-4663-X   (Chivers Large Print)
U.K. Softcover   ISBN 0-7540-4664-8   (Camden Large Print)
U.S. Softcover   ISBN 0-7838-9566-6   (Nightingale Series Edition)

The text of this Large Print edition is unabridged.
Other aspects of the book may vary from the original edition.

Set in 16 pt. New Times Roman.

Printed in Great Britain on acid-free paper.

British Library Cataloguing in Publication Data available

Library of Congress Cataloging-in-Publication Data

Cole, Jackson.
    Hell in paradise / Jackson Cole.
    ISBN 0-7838-9566-6 (lg. print : sc : alk. paper)
    1. Hatfield, Jim (Fictitious character)—Fiction.
    2. Texas Rangers—Fiction. 3. Texas—Fiction. 4. Large type books. I. Title.
    PS3505.O2685 H45 2001
    813'.54—dc21   2001039170

and gents,' Terence Oden was saying, 'and here's Bud Lockhart to give you the details. He's from Acme, that big St. Looey engineerin' firm. Will yuh step up, Lockhart?'

The drone stopped. Lockhart, looking at Lily, wondered why she kept nodding her head toward the platform, a low dais on which the teacher's desk ordinarily stood.

'Meet Bud Lockhart, folks,' said Oden. 'Say, Lockhart, will yuh come here and tell the folks the figgers? Don't be bashful. We ain't got horns like our cattle.'

Lockhart started, ashamed at having been caught daydreaming. He jumped to his feet and shuffled the sheaf of report sheets in his hand importantly. Ranchers, their wives and sons and daughters—the men in range clothing, the women in cotton and gingham— clapped as the engineer took the stand.

Lockhart was a good-looking young fellow, with light hair inclined to curl, and wide-set brown eyes. He wore corduroys tucked into black boots, and a clean khaki shirt covered his broad chest. He had been an athlete at the university he had attended in the East, and now the outdoor life he led as a hydraulic engineer kept him in the pink of condition. The sun had burned his skin a deep tan below the whitish line where his felt hat usually rested on his forehead.

'Delighted to meet all you people,' he said easily, looking at the serious faces lifted to him. He caught Lily Oden's eye, and resolutely looked toward the back of the room. 'Terence Oden and some of the rest of you I've already come to know, and am mighty proud to know. The dam is why I came here. It's necessary to your range. Not only do you need to store water against the dry summer months, but every spring freshet carries off more and more of your top-soil.

'I've learned the history of this section from Hans Vogel and Terence Oden and other pioneers. Of course you all know it was named Dry River because once, long ago, the stream dried up altogether after several years of prolonged drought. I've discovered why the river apparently disappeared, and can prevent it from happening again, I believe. We'll hope to change Dry River's name—by a dam site!'

He waited for the hearty laugh to subside. The pun, which he had used before, always amused such people.

He couldn't help looking again at Lily. There was a a smile in her eyes, and admiration, too, he was sure. He swallowed again, wondering at the lightness of his head, the quick race of his heart beats.

It took him a few moments to open his map of the region and lay out his charts on the teacher's desk, which had been pushed to the wall under the blackboard.

'I've checked your water sources and heard the record of past years,' he said then. 'I have facts and figures to prove that enough water comes from the mountains in the spring freshets to tide you through any possible dry spell, provided it's stored in a properly made dam.'

'Suppose the river goes dry again, young man?'

There was a sardonic note in the heavy voice of the man who spoke, and Lockhart looked at him quickly. He was sitting on the left side of the room, a heavy cane held between his short, dumpy legs, clad in black broadcloth trousers. He had both fat, hairy hands on the top of the thick cane, and was resting his chin on them, as he stared at Lockhart.

Lockhart instinctively disliked the man. He appeared to be a heckler. His body was broad, his head large, and his wide face unpleasant. As he sat there with hunched shoulders, his abbreviated bull neck seemed to have completely disappeared. His head was flat and covered with sparse, lustreless brownish-black hair. His pince-nez jumped as he sniffed loudly through his thick-bridged nose. His lips were thin and rather dark.

As Lockhart framed his reply, he wondered who the man was. He did not appear to be a cowman.

Lockhart had an even temper but the tone of the query had annoyed him. The man seemed to doubt his veracity and ability. He

5

felt a flash of irritation which he sought to keep from his voice, but each word was distinct when he spoke.

'I've told you I can prevent the river from drying up again, sir. It did not actually go dry before. It disappeared into an underground channel for a time. Then the entrance to this tunnel was clogged by earth and rocks carried down by the next spring's flood, which, according to Mr. Vogel, was unusually heavy.'

The questioner wagged his head. 'What about costs, my boy?'

Lockhart felt like a class dunce being given a going over by the teacher. All the other Texans he had met so far had treated him with the deepest kindness, and had showed respect for his technical knowledge. But he kept control over his temper.

'I'll give you the figures,' he said. 'I'd say that by using native soils and stone, the cost will be very reasonable. There's a perfect site for the dam which would require little more than straight construction across a narrow valley neck. The fill would be earth and crushed rock, with a cement breast. The cement will be the only material you will have to import, outside of tools such as scoops, shovels and so on. You have horses and mules on your ranches, and if you get together and pool them for use at the site, it will reduce the cost. I doubt, from what I've seen, if you can scrape up enough native labor hereabouts, but workmen can be brought from El Paso or some other city.'

Lockhart paused to shake out the sketch he had made, and pointed out the advantages of the site he had mentioned.

A rancher got up to ask a question.

'Look here, Oden, our range is free now, ain't it? But when it's irrigated its value'll rise pronto. It'll be fine for farmin' but it won't be so free. How about that?'

'It's a good angle, Baxter,' replied Oden, 'and one we thought of. Our titles are all right, far as our buildin's and filed-on sections go, and we won't need so danged much range per head with water enough and better grass from the irrigation. Every so often there's a bad drought so we lose what we've managed to save up in good years. The water'll put new life in the land, and raise values you say, but to our advantage. The Dry River Cattlemen's Association will control the water—that's us, all together, for the common good.'

The man with the cane spoke up again. 'One important thing, Oden. Who owns the land where our young friend proposes to build this glorified dam?'

'I do.'

An old man with white hair and a seamed red face got up. He was tall and straight in spite of his years, plainly a pioneer rancher. Lockhart knew him, as did all there. He was a Swiss, Hans Vogel, who had come long ago to

7

Dry River. He had emigrated to Texas where he had carved out a home and livelihood for himself. He spoke with an accent, smiling at his neighbors and friends.

'I giff you dis land you need very cheap, boys. I giff it for nudding but better you buy it for a few dollars, Oden and Lockhart say, den dere's no troubles. My wife she iss dead, lige you all know, and I haff no kids. It vill make old Hans glad to help his friends.'

There was applause and Vogel beamed as he sat down, mopping his red face with his bandanna.

'Put it to a vote, Oden,' said a cowman.

Oden called the meeting to order. The Dry River Cattlemen's Association voted for the dam.

'Very good, gentlemen,' said Lockhart. 'I'll go back to the city, report to my company, and work out a detailed operations and cost sheet. I'll catch the morning train out of Kent.'

'One minute!'

The man with the cane rose and turned to the listeners, with the air of an attorney about to present an important case to the jury. He spoke easily, one heavy hand on the cane head, the other draped on the back of his chair.

'With all due respect to our young engineer friend here, I offer you my advice in this matter. If the job of constructing this dam is so simple, why pay a large corporation a lot of good money for it? As a lawyer, I know the ins and outs of such situations. The company has to make a good profit on the job, and profits here and there. Such people as you are usually left holding the short end financially.'

Lockhart bit his lip. He was enraged, and it came out in his voice.

'You mean that my company is unethical enough to profiteer and cheat its clients?' he demanded.

'Just a minute, Lockhart,' Terence Oden interrupted. He frowned as he swung on the lawyer. 'Looka here, Counsellor, we thank yuh for givin' yore advice, only we ain't asked for it or invited yuh here tonight. We're stringin' along with Lockhart and his company. I believe in 'em both. They'll do a good job and it'll be as cheap as possible.'

'Yeah, Sherrall, who asked you to horn in here?' shouted someone not as politely as Oden had spoken.

Boos broke out.

Sherrall shrugged his thick shoulders, gripped his thick cane, and walked out the open door.

'That feller's Luther Sherrall,' Oden said to Lockhart. 'Don't pay any attention to him. He's a lawyer here in town but we won't have no truck with him.'

Lockhart smiled. 'Sorry I lost my temper, Oden.'

Men and women gathered about him,

9

talking with him about the dam, inviting him to come to their homes when he returned. Lily Oden smiled at him, and later, when Oden helped his wife and daughter into the wagon in which they meant to ride back to their home, Lockhart stood in the dusty road to say goodbye.

'I'll be back before long,' he promised.

He stood there, watching them drive off. By the light of the oil lamps in the plaza, he could see Lily still smiling at him as she turned to wave.

Lockhart went to the little boarding-house where he would spend the night. Early the next day he planned to ride south to the town of Kent and the railroad. In his ground floor room that opened on a passageway from Main Street to Tin Can Alley, he quickly fell asleep.

CHAPTER TWO

DEATH DROUGHT

A knife point awoke Lockhart. He recoiled from the sharp pain as it pricked his thigh.

'Be quiet and come weeth me,' a voice whispered. 'Eef you don't, I cut you.'

'Wha-what?' stammered Lockhart, still half-asleep, and sure he was having a vivid nightmare.

'Ssh—not so loud, amigo mio. Pull on boots and pants and come. Pronto.'

'Who are you, anyway?'

The light was dim but he could make out a dark shape topped by a steeple hat. Then teeth and eyes gleamed and a face was turned to him.

'I'm a poor man, little money,' he said, thinking a robber had entered his room. 'Take it and get out.'

'We don't weesh mon-ee from you, senor. Come.'

Lockhart complied. He watched for a chance to fight, to overcome the Mexican. From the soft, slurred words and the general impression he knew the man was a Mexican. But the invader in his room allowed him no opportunity. Besides, he was not only armed with that knife but also wore a revolver.

Ordered out through an open window, to Tin Can Alley, Lockhart traveled for about a block with his alert captor close behind him.

'In zere, senor,' the Mexican said then, indicating an open back door. Lamplight was coming from a front room. Lockhart walked ahead through a short hall, into a square room fitted with a desk, table and chairs, and with straw mats on the floor. The front windows gave out on the plaza, but curtains were drawn over them. On the table was a small kerosene lamp, and by its light the engineer took in the party assembled.

11

Luther Sherrall sat facing Hans Vogel, the old Swiss who had offered to give the cowmen land for their dam. Vogel's face was a deep red. He was an angry man, and his lips were set as he shook his head stubbornly.

'I don't lige you, Counsellor,' he was saying. 'I nefer did lige you. You are not goot man.'

'Keep a civil tongue in yore head, you old he-goat,' ordered a cold-eyed man standing at Vogel's left shoulder. A heavy black beard stubble was on this man's squarish jaw, he had a receding brow and a wide but lipless mouth with a twist to one side. He wore brown leather and a flat-topped 'Nebraska' Stetson. Two walnut-stocked six-shooters rode in his oiled holsters, the belts taut about his burly hips.

'You, Cheyenne Driscoll—you are no goot, either,' growled Vogel.

Now Lockhart had a chance clearly to see the Mexican who had fetched him to Sherrall's office at knife point. He was handsome and lean, with brown, smooth-skinned face and black eyes. A pleasant smile was on his lips. And now Lockhart also could see that besides his knife and gun that a thick-butted black whip hung at his belt by a swivel and snap.

Sherrall looked grim. He glanced at Lockhart and nodded.

'Have him sit down, Enrique,' he said to the Mexican.

'What's the meaning of this, Sherrall?'

12

demanded Lockhart, but Enrique, still smiling, shoved him into a chair.

Sherrall pulled a small silver box from his pocket, extracted a pinch of brownish powder from it, snuffed it from between thumb and forefinger, and sneezed violently. Tears came into his eyes and he wiped his face with his kerchief. He took snuff Lockhart thought so that the discoloration of his lips no doubt came from the habit of chewing it as well as sniffing it.

'My client wants this note paid immediately, Vogel,' said Sherrall coldly. 'You must be getting soft in the head, giving away that land for a song. We can't permit it, since you owe this money.'

'I don't remember dot note at all. I t'ink you are a t'ief, Counsellor, ja. Oden vill help me.'

Sherrall jumped to his feet with an impatient curse.

'Sign this or we'll blow your brains out Vogel!' he snapped.

'Cheyenne' Driscoll drew a Colt, cocked it, and held it to the old man's ear. Sherrall shoved a pen and a bottle of ink over but Vogel still refused to pick up the pen.

Lockhart didn't like the looks of the three who were threatening old Vogel. Driscoll and Enrique would as soon kill a man as blink, he decided, and Sherrall was their leader. He considered Sherrall a poor lawyer, however, because any paper signed with a gun to the

13

head would never be valid and he wished to save Vogel's life.

'You better sign, Hans,' he advised. He tried a quick wink at Vogel.

Vogel was confused, and alarmed as a man might well be, facing such killers. At last he picked up the pen and shakily signed his name at the bottom of the papers Sherrall presented. On one Lockhart saw in printing:

'QUIT-CLAIM DEED.'

Lockhart hoped that they might be let go, once Vogel had signed as Sherrall desired. He was planning how he would collect avengers, come and arrest the trio, a prospect which pleased him mightily. This attorney's viciousness infuriated Lockhart, roused his fighting blood.

Cheyenne Driscoll had lowered his Colt and slid it back into holster, as Vogel began signing. Sherrall had moved over, to indicate with a stubby forefinger where the old rancher should write his name. Enrique stood watching Lockhart, his slim, velvet-clad back to the table.

Suddenly Hans Vogel jumped to his feet. He whipped the chair around, slamming it over Sherrall's head. With a hoarse cry of battle, the old Swiss dashed for the open doorway at the rear.

Luther Sherrall, quickly recovering,

snatched up his thick cane. Lockhart, amazed at Vogel's strength and swiftness in action sprang forward to aid the rancher. There was a sharp explosion. It came from the cane which Sherrall was pointing at Vogel's back.

Vogel threw up both hands and crashed in the entry.

Lockhart was almost upon Sherrall.

'You murderer!' he shouted. 'You've killed him, Sherrall!'

Blood was gushing from a terrifying wound in Vogel's back, between his shoulder-blades. And even as Lockhart cried out against the cold-blooded killing, he realized that he was as good as dead himself. A witness against Sherrall, he could not be permitted to escape.

He raised his fist to attack Sherrall, who was turning upon him, his eyes flaming, his face stony.

Then something whipped like a lashing snake about Lockhart's throat. It cut off his breath, snapped his head back, and pulled him to his knees. Blood trickled from the burned, bruised flesh of his neck.

It took him two or three seconds to recover enough from the shock to see that Enrique had checked him by curling the black whiplash about his throat.

Sherrall and Driscoll were coming toward him, while the Mexican grinned, holding him where he crouched.

CHAPTER THREE

PARADISE

Once there was a Texas Ranger. He was as tough as fence wire and just as quick on the back-snap. He could ride for days on snatches of sleep, and outlast a camel to the next drink. Young women and girls turned and sighed when they saw him ride across the plaza, and outlaws and Apaches turned to hide in the chaparral when they heard he was coming.

His name was William McDowell, and he was still a Ranger. But the years had caught up with him, and while he felt the same as before when it came to men who broke the laws of the great Lone Star State, he could no longer drive his physical being as he had in his distant youth.

Now he was Captain Bill, responsible for the legal behavior of inhabitants across the Pecos in the far-flung empire there. He sat at his desk in Austin Headquarters, pondering the reports and complaints which reached him. Sometimes his way of pondering differed from the accepted fashion, for he would accept and digest bits of information until they suddenly assumed great importance, and seemed to swell within him. Then he would burst out.

He was at the breaking-point this bright

summer morning. The inkwell jumped inches off the oak desk-top as his gnarled fist slammed down. Sulphurous sounds issued from drawn lips. He had made his diagnosis and from long experience his clever mind told him that a drastic operation was imperative.

'Ranger Hatfield!' he bellowed. 'Get him in here!'

An attendant whizzed from the doorway, and presently there came a soft tread outside. A tall man in boots and range clothing entered.

'You want me, Cap'n Bill?' he asked, in a voice with a gentle drawl.

'Yeah, Jim. Have a seat.' McDowell watched as Jim Hatfield, his greatest Ranger, sat down opposite him. 'Seein' you always does me good, Hatfield.'

Jim Hatfield, indeed, was something to see. He stood well over six feet on legs that were long and well-muscled, and accustomed to gripping the barrel ribs of a horse. His shoulders were wide, tapering to a fighting man's narrow hips, where hung blue steel Colts in oiled black holsters. His black hair and bronzed flesh sheened with perfect health, and in him was the controlled, rippling strength of a panther. In repose he carried himself in the fashion of a relaxed panther.

But McDowell knew with what amazing speed of brain and body Hatfield could strike when it was necessary. Gray-green eyes, half-veiled by long lashes, turned to McDowell with a steady, calm light. Hatfield's features were severe, but they were relieved by his generous, wide mouth. Ruthless with evil-doers, the Ranger had a deep pity for and desire to help victims of oppression.

'First,' began McDowell, 'here's a killin'. Hombre name of Hans Vogel, an old Swiss who settled in Reeves County across the Pecos, along with a rancher by the handle of Terence Oden. Vogel's body was found lyin' on the range a few miles outside of Dry River, the nearest town. No apparent motive. Looked like a wanton shootin' by outlaws mebbe. Ain't much law in that section, as yuh savvy, but Sheriff Cordey of Hudspeth rode over and got nowheres.

'Mebbe a couple weeks later I got this, a special letter from Acme Engineers, a big outfit with headquarters in St. Lou. They ask the Rangers to check up on one of their field men named Lockhart. His first name's Robert, but he's always called Bud. They sent him to survey for a dam on Terence Oden's request. Finally they got a wire from Lockhart sayin' the water was too alkaline to be any good and the dam wasn't to be put in, and Lockhart quit 'em, saying he had been made an offer in Mexico and was hurryin' over the Border for the job.

'They figgered this was a queer way to act, but let it go at that. Then they had a telegram

18

from this Oden askin' where was Lockhart, that he'd told 'em he'd be back and give 'em figgers and so on for their dam.

'Third exhibit is this one from Oden to the Rangers. He can't say exactly what, but there's somethin' fishy goin' on about this consarned dam, which seems to me to be at the bottom of this trouble, Jim.'

Hatfield nodded. 'Looks like it, Cap'n. I reckon this Lockhart was either dry-gulched, like Vogel, and his body ain't been found yet, or else he could have crossed Oden somehow. Have to make shore what sort of Injun Lockhart is before I can say.' The tall man studied the various reports. 'Looks like the dam has been started, Cap'n, from what Oden's latest message says. But the cowmen ain't in on it.'

'Yuh better get right over there to Dry River and smell out what holds, Jim,' said Captain Bill. 'This here request from Missouri has to be too mighty serious. We got to uphold our state's reputation and the Rangers' name with it. Can't have folks sayin' we don't enforce the law here and that Texas ain't safe.'

*   *   *

A little later, McDowell watched Hatfield mount his horse and move away on the run to Dry River. Goldy, the magnificent golden sorrel, stepped proudly as he carried his big

19

rider. In the saddle-bags were iron rations, while under a long leg rode a Winchester carbine in its socket, and a spare belt of ammunition was hanging from the horn.

'Texas never seen a better man,' muttered McDowell, as he stared after the stalwart horseman. 'If it's to be done, Hatfield'll do it!'

It was a highly responsible position that McDowell held. He was in the same situation as a commanding officer in war, forced to order men into the face of death. He never dispatched one of his Rangers without feeling it deeply, for there was always the chance a man might never return from his mission but die in the wilderness under outlaw guns. And McDowell loved them all with a father's devotion . . .

Hatfield's ride, before he crossed the Pecos was a long one, but finally he reached a settlement that cracked under the beating summer sun. Dust lay inches thick in the road and the bushes in the plaza were brown and parched. The heat drew all the moisture from everything, and the little river on which the town stood looked as though it might live up to its name, for the main stream was only a yard in width, and the stones and mud in its bed had dried out.

There were several stores, the only large one a general groceries and feed supplies store, with a drygoods and ranch tools as a sideline. There was a livery stable and a corral, a few board and adobe brick houses, with the awnings of many extending over the sidewalk, and railed for use as second-floor porches. A shingle hanging over a door opposite where Hatfield drew rein read:

LUTHER SHERRALL: ATT'Y AT LAW
Legal Advice and Land Deeds

A man wearing a flat-topped 'Nebraska' hat was lounging beneath the sign. Hatfield called out a question to him.

'Say, ain't this the town of Dry River?'

The burly native son waved a dirty, hairy hand toward a thirty-foot strip of canvas stretched over the road between two tall cedar poles. Red letters on it screamed:

WELCOME TO PARADISE!

The man Hatfield had addressed was the first person he had seen for miles. Most of the townsmen were indoors, keeping as cool as possible or having an after-dinner siesta.

'Can't yuh read, feller?' inquired the burly man. 'Does that look like it said Dry River—or all them other ones?'

There were numerous smaller banners, and cardboard signs in the same hospitable vein.

'I can see it says this is heaven, but that ain't the place I figgered I was headed for,' drawled the Ranger, looking more closely at his informant.

The man wore brown leather pants and a sweated blue shirt. Walnut-stocked six-guns rode at his hips. He needed a shave, for his square jaw was bristling with black stubble, and his wide, lipless mouth was twisted to one side. The eyes raised to the mounted Ranger were fish-blue and cold.

'My handle is Cheyenne Driscoll,' he said. 'What can I do for yuh?'

Hatfield felt that the fellow was not only tough, but shrewd as well. It was the Ranger's habit to look carefully at a situation before making known his identity, and he did not intend to start out this job by exposing his hand. Well-organized robbers usually kept alert and on guard, and the fact that Cheyenne Driscoll was on the street, the only man in town braving the sun, made him wary—to say nothing of the burly fellow's face.

'My name is Jim Hays,' the Ranger said. 'I'm a cowman from the Nueces and I'd been figgerin' on startin' another spread in these parts. But I don't know as this country'll do. It seems all-fired dry.'

Cheyenne Driscoll's frozen face melted into a grin.

'Glad to meet yuh, Hays. Don't let the dryness worry yuh none. Yuh must've heard we're buildin' a big dam and we guarantee water year in, year out. It'll be finished before long. I was only foolin' yuh, pardner. This town used to be called Dry River but we done changed its handle to Paradise, 'count of that's what it'll be when irrigated. C'mon in and have a drink.'

Hatfield dismounted, led the golden sorrel to the shady side of the building, and dropped his reins. His spurs tinkled as he followed Cheyenne Driscoll into a nearby one-storied adobe brick building with a flat roof. It was a square building and evidently had been designed for a store. Over the door a fresh-painted sign said:

PARADISE LAND & WATER CO.
LUTHER SHERRALL, PRES.

In the front room, which was large and oblong, were chairs and tables, and a desk on which were three ink bottles, pens, and piles of bright-colored papers. On the wall spaces between the open windows were large maps of Dry River—now Paradise—sections.

In violent blue a great lake stood out, obviously to be formed by the projected dam, with blue lines radiating from the main body of water to mark irrigation canals. Lots had been marked off and numbered, while several were inscribed 'Sold.'

The artist had let his fancy roam and had embellished the maps with pictures of men plowing rich black earth, of high stands of wheat and corn, of roomy, handsome

23

ranchhouses and cowmen lolling at ease in the shade of giant trees. Everybody was happy in the paintings. On the tables were pitchers of water, glasses, and whisky in bottles. A couple of quiet-eyed men, unobtrusively wearing Colts in their holsters, and dressed in dark clothing, lounged in the rear.

Behind the desk was a broad-bodied personage with short, thick limbs and a large head covered with dull, brownish-black hair. He wore a pince-nez on the bridge of his thick nose and as he looked up at the tall visitor whom Cheyenne Driscoll had escorted in, the glasses jumped with his sudden, violent snuffing. His lips were thin, stained, blue-black.

'Snuff,' decided the Ranger. 'Rubs it in his gums, too.' The habit was popular in some districts.

They were all watching him, and he assumed the friendly manner of a stranger in a new country. During his investigations he was often called on to pose as other than a lawman, and he had a flair for it. He had traveled widely and knew the speech and characteristics of the inhabitants of many sections.

An opening led to the back of the building. On that wall were more maps and idealistic portrayals of Paradise as it was to be. One which occupied a full panel and extended for several feet showed a thriving, beautiful little city filled with imposing white structures and peopled with smiling, well-to-do citizens. There were gleaming new stores and business blocks, a tree- and flower-laden plaza, and fine residences on the outskirts. Beyond was the sweep of green range on which fed contented cattle owned, obviously, by the wealthy ranchers who lived in the great haciendas indicated.

The title of this artist's dream was 'PARADISE.' A sub-heading read, 'And the Desert Shall Blossom as the Rose.'

'Mighty arty, ain't it?' said Cheyenne fondly, as he saw Hatfield staring at the picture.

'Shore is.'

Hatfield nodded his appreciation.

CHAPTER FOUR

RIDDLES

Gazing at the pictured landscape, Jim Hatfield's keen eyes were all-seeing enough to catch a sudden glint from a dark spot marking a window in one of the painted buildings. Then it was gone, but he heard a faint rustling, and decided that observers must be posted behind thin paneling set up to partition off the large store. What he had glimpsed had been light shining on a human eyeball. Someone had peeked through at him, and no doubt there were other such peep-holes.

'Say, Sherrall,' Cheyenne Driscoll said, 'this there is Jim Hays, from the Nueces country. He's lookin' for rangeland up thisaway, and I was tellin' him he shore come to the right place.'

'How do you do, sir—how do you do!' Sherrall's heavy voice was tuned to a sugar-coated, hearty pitch in which a businessman might greet a prospective customer. He smiled widely, showing stained teeth and bluish gums. The hand that was thrust out to shake Hatfield's was hairy, and the grip strong.

'Yes, Cheyenne is right,' he said. 'You've come to the right place. How much range were you thinking of purchasing?'

'Well, if it's good I might start with six sections. I'd like to begin in a small way over here, since I'm set up already at home. Sort of thought I'd branch out some, and try selective breedin', that new-fangled idea that's come out.'

'Very interesting—very.' Sherrall liked to repeat his thought, to emphasize his speech.

Hatfield stood a foot taller than the president of the Paradise Land & Water Company, but Sherrall was almost as heavy, with his abnormally thick thighs and upper arms. A stout cane leaned on the side of his desk.

He led Hatfield to the big map. 'This spot here, now—it's in the foot-hills southwest of the dam. Good protection in the winter—yes, excellent protection. Just the thing for your breeding idea, sir. You have a chance now to gain a share of water stock for each section purchased. That's for a few days, because it's limited. We're doing it for a few favored customers.' Sherrall beamed, sniffed.

'On the map it looks all right,' Hatfield said. 'Of course I'd like to see it before I put my money in, Sherrall.'

'Of course—only common sense, of course.' Sherrall drew a small silver box from his pocket and pressed a spring-snap which sent the cover jumping open. It was filled with pulverized tobacco, and he held it out to the Ranger. 'Do you indulge, Hays?'

'No, thanks.'

'Excuse me, then.'

Sherrall took a pinch of the brown powder between thumb and forefinger, held it to his nostrils with a dainty gesture, snuffed deeply. Water came to his eyes, and he sniffed and sneezed violently. He wiped his face with a silk kerchief.

'Do you smoke cigars? Please help yourself.' He held an open box out. The Ranger accepted one and lighted up. 'A drink? How about a drink? Best whisky west of the Pecos.'

'Don't care if I do, Sherrall.'

Hatfield was now sitting opposite Sherrall at

the desk. Soon he found he was reading the prospectus. He puffed faster and faster on his cigar. Whoever had written the thing was a master painter too, with words. 'Shore sounds promisin'!' he exclaimed. To himself he mused, 'Dog it, if I wasn't leery of the whole set-up, and I had any money, I'd shore give it to 'em!'

'You see, we guarantee to buy back your land at any time within two years after you occupy it, in case it doesn't satisfy you, Hays,' explained Sherrall gravely. 'You can't lose.'

There were many 'ifs,' 'buts,' 'in case ofs,' and other modifications, and Hatfield grew lost in the maze. He went back to the beginning, trying to figure it all out. That prospectus gave him a glowing impression of huge profits to be made if he bought now, before the whole world and his son surged to Paradise to live happily ever after.

'Our company is sponsored by that philanthropic statesman, Senator Madison Baggett, who stands behind all statements we make!' declared Sherrall.

Hatfield knew considerable about the Senator's good reputation.

He was roused from his study of the prospectus by a low but urgent clucking made by Cheyenne Driscoll's tongue. Glancing up, he found that Driscoll was frowning, nodding at the front window. As he looked, Cheyenne framed an 'O' with his mouth.

28

Sherrall seized his cane and held it in his hands.

'Hays,' he said, 'Driscoll'll run you up so you can see that section.' Sherrall was in a hurry, wanting to get him out of there.

'What's that?' he asked, purposely obtuse.

'C'mon, let's take a ride,' urged Driscoll.

Out of the corner of his eye, Hatfield caught Sherrall's hand signal to men hidden behind the panel. Something was up, and he did not wish to miss it.

'I'd kind of like to finish my readin', Sherrall,' he drawled, 'and the cigar. It's mighty hot, and my hoss is tired. Thought I'd wait till it cools some this afternoon. Have you any other spots I might like?'

He talked on, delaying them. He only needed a couple of minutes; and as Driscoll glanced indecisively at Sherrall, a dozen riders pulled up in a cloud of dust and came barging into the office.

Hatfield read calmly on, as though he had not noticed anything:

—an easy life in the unfailing fair sun of the greatest state in our glorious Union, a land of milk and honey, blessed by every possible advantage. Where children grow to manhood without thoughts of ills or cares, where fond parents indulge, bestowing every luxury upon their offspring and themselves!

29

Water, clean and cool, from mountain springs iced by the soft caress of Nature. Water for your home, your stock, for swimming pool and fish pond, water to grow forests and grass higher than a cow's horns, piped wherever you wish by gravity! Life-giving water on which all depend is offered you in limitless amounts by Paradise, and truly this *is* paradise but attainable *now* by those fortunate enough to—

Hatfield blew forth a cloud of bluish cigar smoke and looked up again from the prospectus as a lean, somber Texan with crisp gray hair and a wiry black mustache bristling over his grim mouth, burst in the door and faced Luther Sherrall with fire in his dark-blue eye.

'Well, Oden, what do you want now?' demanded Sherrall coldly. 'I'm very busy at the moment. Can't you come back later?'

'I'm here and I'll have my say, Sherrall.'

The man Sherrall called Oden wore two six-shooters. His leather pants and blue shirt and half-boots were dusty from a ride. The men behind him were cowboys and ranchers, all armed. A couple of them carried shotguns at the ready.'

'This'll be Terence Oden,' thought the Ranger. He was alert and interested, as he listened and watched.

Cheyenne Driscoll's manner had changed as

Oden entered. He had forgotten all about the customer, and so had Sherrall. They glared at Oden. The Ranger was thoughtful as he got up and went over to the window at the other side of the room, out of line with the holes in the panel painting. He had heard new rustlings behind him.

Driscoll's eyes were slitted and his lips were twisted in a snarl. His hands hung limp, close to the butts of his guns, and he never took his eye off Oden. However, Driscoll also placed himself out of the direct line of any fire from the rear.

'You savvy why we're here, Sherrall,' snapped Oden. 'Yuh took over our idea and got holt of Vogel's land. Yore men are throwin' up that dam we planned, but we can't get anywheres near the site. Armed guards hold us off.'

'You're a trouble-maker, Oden,' declared Sherrall, in an injured tone. 'I informed you that Christian Vogel, Hans' nephew, is my client. Christian held notes for a large amount he had loaned his uncle long ago. To protect his interests, he had a signed quit-claim deed to Vogel's properties, including the dam site. I have only protected my client's interests. When Christian learned that his uncle had gone soft-headed and was throwing all his substance to the four winds, he requested me to step in and save what I could.'

'I knowed Hans Vogel for thirty years, and

31

he never mentioned no nephew Christian,' said Oden. His voice had a sardonic ring as he added, 'Mebbe Hans forgot!'

'It's quite possible since he was obviously failing in mind as well as body,' replied Sherrall in his cold, heavy tone. He called: 'Vogel! Will you step in here, please?'

A man in a dark suit came through the doorway at the back. He was about forty, round of head, and his face was as full as a harvest moon. His chin was receding, his eyes brown.

'You vant me, Counsellor?' he asked wildly.

'Yes, Vogel. These men doubt your existence.' Sherrall's words dripped virulent sarcasm to match Oden's. 'Oden, this is Christian Vogel, Hans' nephew. My client. I have in my safe the quit-claim deed to all Hans Vogel's lands, signed and sealed by Hans, and also the signed, uncanceled notes he gave to Christian. I will show them at the proper time, in case you force me. But I warn you, it'll cost you money to see them in court.'

Oden was plainly nonplussed. 'Yuh're Hans' nephew, mister?' he asked.

'Ja. He was my uncle. A goot man. I come from Kansas when Counsellor Sherrall wire me, ja.' Vogel beamed.

For a time as Oden stood there silently, the Ranger thought he looked foolish. The rancher turned to his friends then, and they whispered together.

'After all, Oden,' Sherall took the opportunity to say, 'you fellows will be able to enjoy the water as much as any new settlers. When the dam's finished, the Company'll gladly furnish you with it.'

'That's so, Oden,' said one of the cowmen. 'We can still irrigate our range.'

The tension relaxed.

'We're taking all the risk,' Sherrall continued, 'making the investment in money and materials and time to build the dam for you.'

Oden scratched his head. 'How much yuh chargin' us?' he inquired at last. He slammed a tight fist into his palm, making a sound like a pistol crack.

Sherrall essayed a faint, condescending smile. 'That's impossible to say at this time. It depends on the final costs of the dam, the number of settlers, what the pro rata charge to each customer of the Water Company must be.'

'Huh. And the company bein' yores, Sherrall, it all depends on you!' Oden's face hardened again. 'There's a couple other little puzzles need to be cleared up too, and it might as well be now. How yuh explain Vogel dyin' so handy-like, just before his nephew showed up? And what have yuh done with young Bud Lockhart, that Acme engineer? His firm says they ain't heard a word from him and can't trace him.' Oden lifted his voice and shouted,

'I reckon the Texas Rangers'll be interested in them things!'

The set-up grew clearer to Jim Hatfield. Oden and the other ranchers had planned the dam. Luther Sherrall had strong-armed his way in, decided Hatfield, had taken it over, was putting it through so that he held control. Money was rolling in from sale of land and of water stock. With this cash Sherrall could operate, hire his labor, and the protective employees he probably considered he needed.

And Oden had put his finger on the kernel of the matter. Once Sherrall had the settlers hooked and on their land, his Water Company could charge whatever the traffic would bear. A large fortune could be cleaned up, by legal means, within a short period.

CHAPTER FIVE

NEW CUSTOMER

Sherrall was angry. The hot blood that flushed his cheeks showed in blotches on his unhealthy skin.

'Are you threatening me, Oden?' he demanded of the rancher leader. 'I warn you I'll exercise my inalienable right as an American to defend myself. You can air your fancied grievances in the courts.' Sherrall was gripping his thick cane as he glared at Oden.

'The courts?' Oden laughed shortly. 'I savvy a slimy eel can't be easy held. The only way is to step on such a critter's head and crush it. Yuh been too quick for me, Sherrall, but one of these days I'll come up with yuh.'

Oden bristled, stepping close to Sherrall's desk. His fists were doubled tight, and he shook one under the lawyer's nose.

Sherrall thrust back his chair as he rose to his feet. A flash of alarm flickered in his muddy eyes, and he sniffed violently.

'Get out of this office and stay away from my properties, Oden!' he shouted. 'I've had enough of your insolence.'

The Ranger got ready. He had a plan of action in mind. He could blast that beautiful idealistic painting of Paradise town, and throw off the hidden marksmen. This would give Oden and the men with him a couple of seconds in which to duck from the room.

Cheyenne Driscoll stood between Hatfield and the group of cowmen. Oden had moved into the space before the desk, but it would be dangerous for those behind the wall to open up. They would probably hit their boss if they did. However, Cheyenne jumped in and rammed a swiftly drawn Colt into Oden's spine, just as the enraged rancher had drawn back his fist as though to punch Sherrall in the face.

'Hold yore hosses, Oden, or I'll blow yore back through yore yeller middle, cuss yuh!'

Driscoll swore at the rancher in the most picturesque Border profanity.

'Don't shoot, boys!' ordered Oden.

He pulled himself back, gaining some self-control. The men he led had started to draw, and there would have been a bloody melee had not Oden checked it.

Hatfield, ready for the scrap, wondered if Oden might not be aware of the hidden gunmen back of the screen. The rancher glanced that way, then nodded and slowly turned to leave the office, his friends grouped about him.

Driscoll, at a shake of Sherrall's head, subsided, allowing Oden to go. There were several good reasons, thought Ranger, why Sherrall hadn't opened the ball. First, he might have been afraid of being hit in the action. Second, he evidently disliked open warfare, for his mind was a devious one. And third, there was a customer watching the show.

Sherrall leaned his cane against the wall as the ranchers, outside, hit leather and turned to ride out of town. He extracted his snuff-box, daintily pinched up the pulverized tobacco between thumb and forefinger, sniffed it and sneezed two or three times, once more wiping his face with his silk handkerchief.

He smiled and nodded to the tall man on the opposite side of the room.

'Sorry this had to happen while you were here, Hays. That Oden fellow is a stupid oaf. You know when a man gets an idea which seems about to pay dividends there are always dishonest characters who try to claim it as their own and cash in by foul tactics. Oden's a notorious liar and troublemaker in these arts.'

'He needs the right kind of persuadin', Sherrall,' growled Cheyenne, his nostrils still flared in fighting fury. But he subsided as Sherrall frowned at him.

'Suppose you take our friend Hays to Golden Gates and set them up,' Sherrall suggested. 'He may want a bite to eat, too, Cheyenne. You can introduce him to Jervis, and let them get acquainted. Jervis is another prospective buyer, Hays. He probably will have the section next to yours. He came in this morning. You can all go out together . . . Cheyenne, while Hays and Jervis are having a drink together, you step back here. I have something to say to you.'

'All right, Boss. C'mon, Hays.'

Hatfield hesitated. He was acting the part of the innocent bystander and customer.

'Look here, Sherrall,' he said. 'If there's any fuss about the title to that land, I ain't interested.'

'Title's clean as a whistle,' declared Sherrall. 'Why, I give you a written warranty and guarantee! Just let Driscoll show you the property. You can have your own lawyer check

37

up.'

'Well, all right. But that Oden acts like a right salty hombre. I ain't honin' to buy a peck of trouble.'

'Forget Oden. Let me worry about that.'

Hatfield went up the street with Cheyenne Driscoll to a large saloon with a new sign— 'Golden Gates.' No doubt Sherrall had rechristened it to match the name of the town.

It was cooler inside, because of the damp sawdust on the floor. There were tables and chairs, a bar along the side wall fitted with shining glasses and bottles in rows, and two barkeepers. A scattering of citizens stood here, drinking. Driscoll hailed a middle-aged man with graying hair and a trusting, innocent face.

'How yuh doin', Jervis? Meet Jim Hays. He means to buy up six sections next yours. In a lettle while I'll run you boys up for a look-see. Meantime, excuse me, I'm goin' back to the office.'

Hatfield found Jervis just what he appeared to be—a retired merchant whose hobby had been cattle raising and farming. Now he wished to take it up in a small way, for his health, and he meant to invest his savings in the Paradise scheme. He was rather deaf, and in order to converse with him, Hatfield had to shout. After some minutes of this noisy small-talk, the Ranger yelled:

'I'm goin' in back and wash up, Jervis. Order another on me.'

'What's that? You say yore mother ran somewhere?' asked the deaf Jervis, his mild eyes troubled.

A bartender grinned at Hatfield.

'Set 'em up, Jake,' Hatfield said to the barkeep. He made motions to Jervis and went quickly through a back curtain.

There was a door marked 'Gents,' which the Ranger passed on his way to Tin Can Alley. In a few steps he was at the passage leading by Sherrill's north windows to the street. There was an open window in the rear, beneath which he ducked low in passing. Then he heard Sherrall's voice coming through the opening near-by, and pushed close to the whitewashed wall.

'—sick of Oden,' finished the lawyer in angry tones.

'Why'd yuh stop me'n the boys from gunnin' the skunks, then?' asked Cheyenne.

'It would have been stupid unless they forced it. In broad daylight, with Hays a witness? We'd have lost our customer, for one thing, and it would have been dangerous at such close range. No, we can handle the rest, once Oden's out of the way. He's the ringleader.'

'I'll get him tonight,' Cheyenne said confidently.

'Take plenty of men along,' advised Sherrall, 'and above all, don't be seen or caught. Wait till the Dot O quiets down—say

39

eleven or twelve o'clock, when they're all asleep. A knife would be better than a gun, too, unless you can knock Oden out and do the job in the mesquite out of hearing. I'd rather have him found on the range, if possible.'

'Like Vogel?'

Sherrall sniffed, then sneezed. Hatfield knew he had just taken snuff.

Suddenly the Ranger realized that three men, with Colts prominent in their belts, had appeared at the end of the building, and one pointed at him, dropping a hand to a gun.

Hatfield was not ready to expose his hand, and he was at a disadvantage, caught in the narrow alleyway between the road and where the trio of Sherrall's men stood.

'Oh, Sherrall!' he sang out boldly. 'Hey, Cheyenne!'

He thrust his head and shoulders through the window opening. It was just by Sherrall's desk, and the startled attorney and Driscoll quit talking to stare at him. The gunmen in the alley held their fire, watching.

'What yuh doin' there, Hays?' demanded Cheyenne suspiciously.

'I forgot to see to my hoss, boys. He's plumb wore out and he's a fine one. Is there a livery stable handy?'

'Yeah,' replied Driscoll. 'Right across plaza. We'll lend yuh a nag to ride this afternoon.'

'Gracias. I'm ready any time yuh say. That

Jervis is a right nice hombre, ain't he?' Hatfield beamed upon them.

His talk seemed to quell any rising suspicion they might have entertained, and they had their eye on his supposed wealth. He went to the street, picked up Goldy, and led the sorrel over to the stable to have him rubbed down and taken care of.

'Turn him into that corral when yuh're through, boy,' he ordered the wrangler.

'Si, senor.' The Mexican lad grinned as he caught the silver dollar the Ranger tossed him.

Hatfield saw where his saddle was hung. He helped rub down the sorrel, but before they had finished, he heard Cheyenne Driscoll calling him. Jervis and the gunman were ready to go, and there was a rangy black mustang waiting for the tall man. Hatfield mounted and, with Cheyenne gaily chatting, they rode northwest from Paradise.

As they climbed a gentle slope out of the river valley, the grass and bush grew brown. It was withered in the drought.

'Mighty dry country,' observed Hatfield, with a shake of his head.

'No,' replied Jervis, 'I ain't goin' to buy this, Hays. The section I picked is near yores.'

Cheyenne winked at the Ranger.

'At least yuh won't have to worry if yuh like to yodel, Hays,' he said, sotto voce. 'It won't bother Jervis none.'

'I ain't worried about Jervis,' Hatfield said

41

soberly. 'It's that Oden hombre. I hope his spread ain't near mine. He seems quarrelsome.'

Driscoll stopped smiling.

'The Dot O lies up that north road branch, Hays,' he said steadily. 'It's five mile from yore site. And as for Oden—forget the skunk. He'll bother nobody.'

CHAPTER SIX

THE DAM SITE

The river came from brown-crested hills which terraced into the north and west. A heat haze hung over them. From high points on the road the approaching riders could see sweeps of range, with here and there a bunch of steers browsing on the burnt grasses.

Driscoll pointed to a small frame house of native timber standing on the river bank.

'That's Vogel's place,' he explained. 'His nephew's takin' over soon, now that the old man is dead. The Dot O's out of sight behind them hills.'

The dirt and rock trail curved. Higher, rocky shoulders formed an upper valley. Apparently they came together at the south terminus, but when the riders drew closer they saw a narrow gap. It was at this point, with the valley widening behind it in roughly oval shape, and the river meandering along the bottom, that the dam was being built.

They saw raw gashes, red clay and gray rocks. Tents and crude shacks stood outside the gap on the flat to the west, and smoke curled up from two fires. Horses drawing scoops, laborers with barrows, shovels and picks, swarmed about the site. The stream had been diverted to one side, an easy matter with the water so low.

'We're well along,' said Cheyenne.

The vista was cut off as they descended into the outer valley in order to reach the camp. Crossing the almost dry bed of the muddied stream, the three dusty riders pushed their horses to the west bank. A man with a double barreled, sawed-off shotgun stepped from behind some high boulders.

'Howdy, Cheyenne,' he said.

'Howdy, Smoke,' replied Driscoll. 'These gents are Hays and Jervis, goin' to buy some of them upper sections.'

Hatfield took in the sentry's lean, shrewd face. He wore dark leather pants, a green shirt and Stetson. A Colt .45 hung at his thigh.

'Better let Enrique savvy yuh're comin', Cheyenne,' advised this man whom Driscoll had called 'Smoke.' 'There was a couple hoss thieves lurkin' 'round last night.'

'That's easy,' said Driscoll.

He drew his six-shooter and fired a one-two

signal which reverberated through the warm air.

Moving on, the Ranger was aware that the road was carefully guarded. He saw three more sentries, who passed them with a wave of the hand.

'Mebbe more who didn't show,' Hatfield decided. 'It'd be hard to come in on a hoss without usin' this trail, too.'

When they came into the camp at the dam, more armed men were around. Up the line, laborers toiled at filling in the gap, shored up with timbers and logs. Stores stood under sheds—food and equipment. The fires were for cooking, and for an open-air forge.

'Looks fine, hey, boys?' sang out Cheyenne cheerily. 'C'mon and we'll see that land yuh're goin' to buy.'

Hatfield was interested in the dam. He always was interested in such things, for he had studied engineering for two years, before the death of his father had sent him to become a Texas Ranger.

'I'll mosey up the line, Cheyenne,' he said, 'and see what she's like.'

He swung his horse before Driscoll could make objection, and rode toward the dam.

There was a beaten path up from the site into some cedar woods. The Ranger thought he made out part of a wooden palisades through the trees. But as he climbed the slope toward it, a tall Mexican stepped out and grinned up at him, white teeth flashing.

'Es nozzing up zere, beeg senor. You go back.'

He wore a steeple hat trimmed with silver conchas, a purple silk shirt and tight-fitting bell-shaped pants. He was handsome, with his smooth skin, dark eyes and gleaming white teeth. He wore the usual knife, and at his wide expensive leather belt, studded with large silver circles, hung a thick-butted black whip.

'Just lookin' around, vaquero,' Hatfield shrugged. 'I aim to buy some land near here if it's all right.'

'Si, ees fine. You mak' mon-ees, si.'

The Ranger's curiosity was aroused. He wondered why the handsome Mexican kept him from investigating the pine woods. To make sure, he tried to push the black horse past, around the fellow in the trail. A brown hand shot out and seized the bridle strap, jerked the mustang around none too gently. The smile was still on the Mexican's lips as he slapped the black's haunch and sent him sliding down the path.

'I see you again, beeg senor,' he called.

In his role as a rancher hunting land, Hatfield could not press too closely without losing his advantage. He rejoined Driscoll, who had followed him, and was frowning.

'Reckon I was too nosey, Cheyenne,' he observed with a grin. 'That Mexican turned me back.'

'Huh. That's Enrique. He's boss here and what he says goes.' After a minute, Driscoll added, 'I guess mebbe they caught them hoss thieves and didn't want yuh to see 'em hangin'. Yeah, that's it.'

Cheyenne was in a hurry to get them away from the camp, and Jervis and the Ranger followed him until they came out below the dam site, where for some miles rolling land covered by sered bunch grasses and mesquite could be seen.

'This is it, boys,' announced Driscoll. 'Look her over. Ain't it beautiful?' He cocked a leg up and reached for the 'makin's.'

'Mighty dry,' said Jervis, shaking his head.

'That mesquite'll have to be cut off,' declared Hatfield wisely. 'It ruins a range.'

'Water'll feed this land by gravity from the lake,' said Cheyenne. 'All you need. Then the grass'll stay emerald green all year.'

The two customers got down, Jervis knelt, to take the soil in his hand and let it trickle through his fingers. He and Hatfield walked around for a time, then remounted and rode slowly, looking at the land.

Cheyenne humored them, but he was impatient to return to Paradise. When Jervis was satisfied, they headed for town by a short-cut south of the spot where the dam was being thrown up, and by dusk were in the Golden Gates, to wet their dry throats. More citizens had emerged after the heat of the day had

46

subsided. There was a piano player and violinist torturing their instruments in the Annex, and some girls were whirling in the dance with those who had the energy for such amusement.

Luther Sherrall, leaning on his thick cane, smiled and slapped the two prospects heartily on the back as Cheyenne piloted them to him. 'How did you like it? Wonderful, isn't it? . . . Eddie, set them up for these two gentlemen. Their money's no good here—it's all on me. Have some hot supper served at once.'

'I'm willin' to throw in with yuh Sherrall,' Jervis nodded.

'Me, too,' Hatfield also nodded. 'Though I'd like a day or two to think it over. I'll hang round town and see about transferrin' some funds from Houston. I like to pay cash.'

'Splendid!' Sherrall beamed through the thick pince-nez. The glasses bobbed as he sniffed.

Cheyenne Driscoll, having swallowed two long drinks in record time, said:

'I'll sashay now, gents. Good luck. See yuh tomorrer.'

'A busy little bee,' mused Hatfield. 'Takes care of customers all day, then he has night work at the Dot O.'

Aloud he asked, 'Yuh say the land's sellin' well, Sherrall?'

'Couldn't ask for more. Senator Madison Baggett, who is sponsoring our company, is at

47

present on a tour to carry the good news throughout the state. A great statesman and orator, the Senator.'

Sherrall bobbed his head with the deepest admiration. 'I want you to meet him, Hays. He'll be along in a few days. And you mustn't miss the big party we intend to have soon. We're bringing in hundreds on an excursion train to Kent and thence to Paradise by team. The Senator will speak and there'll be barbecues, music, and a wonderful time for all.'

After a hearty meal and several drinks—charged to Sherrall's account—the tall Ranger gravely shook hands, thanking the attorney for his hospitality.

'I'll be turnin' in,' he said. 'I'm plumb wore out from ridin' and the excitement. See yuh in the mornin'.'

He turned in, stretching out on a bunk in a converted barn across the alley from the saloon's rear entry. Jervis slept there, too. Sherrall kept it for guests, prospects staying at Paradise to invest in water stock or in land.

It was a simple matter for Hatfield, a little later when Jervis was snoring, to tiptoe out a side door, and head for the corral where Goldy was kept. He saddled up, not disturbing the sleeping boy at the stable, and left the settlement by a back route. That day he had learned the approximate location of the Dot O from Cheyenne, and it had been marked on the maps of the region he had studied.

The Ranger rode in silver moonlight that outlined the winding road. Mesquite and other native growth cast inky shadows across his path. Driscoll and his force must be ahead of him in the night, and Hatfield meant to warn Terence Oden.

'We'll have to look over that camp by the dam when they ain't expectin' us,' he informed Goldy. 'That may not be so open-and-shut as this job.'

Near ten P.M. he saw lights in a large house ahead. The country was fairly open, broken only by small stands of woods and mesquite clumps, with a few outcroppings, so that he could see to leave the road to circle around. Dropping his reins in a patch of trees, he checked his Colts and started on foot toward the ranchhouse.

The lights were in the front of the big house. The rear was dark, and he chose this approach, beginning his stalk well out, keeping low and off the sky line and moving with an Apache crawl. When he stopped, he lay flat along the shadowed side of a square tool shed about twenty-five yards from the main building.

His eyes sought to pierce the gloom beyond the patches of yellow light which came from the open windows. As he watched, a silent figure moved slowly against one of these, going toward the back of the place. For an instant he thought perhaps the enemy had already struck, but the measured tread passed on and around the end of the building.

'Sentry,' he decided. 'Oden's got savvy.'

Save for the armed guard patrolling the grounds, the Dot O was undisturbed.

'They ain't hit, yet,' Hatfield mused. 'It's Oden they're after, and Sherrall ordered 'em to make it quiet.'

He settled himself for a long wait. Half an hour passed, then another. The rest was not unpleasant, as the tall officer had made a swift run to Paradise, with but snatches of sleep.

'Must be eleven o'clock,' he thought, as he watched the sentry round his side of the ranch.

The cowboy guard took about ten minutes to make a full circuit. He would pause now and then to look out into the moonlit spaces beyond the trees and brush shading the home.

The glow in the front room suddenly was reduced. Someone had turned the lamp down.

Hatfield could still see the guard. The pacing waddy, a shotgun in his hand, seemed going about his duties as regular as clockwork. The Ranger observed him as he disappeared past the kitchen entry. Chin resting on his hands as he lay flat on his stomach, Hatfield waited for the sentry to round the front veranda again.

He grew mildly surprised when the cowboy failed to appear on the minute he was due, but figured the fellow might have paused for a smoke. He had heard nothing to make him believe the guard was being changed. When the sentinel was overdue by ten minutes, the Ranger moved slightly, listening, peering at the faint illuminations which came from the low-burning oil lamp inside the ranchhouse.

A pebble clacked against another, at his right, off in the flowering shrubs, part of the concealment he had himself made use of in approaching the tool shed. He froze, his face shielded from the light. Someone was creeping toward him, foot by foot.

There had been no alarm, nothing to tell him his foes were there. But from the corner of one eye he sighted the darker shadow bellying toward him.

The Ranger tensed, ready to strike. The man's hand, extended to feel the ground ahead, touched his shoulder, and he recoiled, with startled shock.

'Yuh're in the wrong place, Tiny!' he whispered hoarsely. 'Cheyenne told me to cover from here. The boys got the sentry on the other side. Let's go in.'

With the man who had crept up believing the one lying by the shed was one of his own party, it was easy for the Ranger. His long-fingered hands, with the power of a steel vise in them, gripped the fellow's throat. Cries were shut off, dying in the constricted windpipe. Holding him down with his weight, Hatfield throttled him until he relaxed, only a few brushing sounds of leather against the earth telling of the tussle.

CHAPTER SEVEN

NIGHT FORAY

Hatfield drew a Colt and cocked the hammer back under his thumb. He began crawling toward the corner of the house. He moved as quickly as he could, and against a faint beam from a front window saw another shadow pushing in. To his left he heard more men.

They had disposed of the waddy skillfully, without any alarm to the ranch, and were on the way in to take Oden.

Sure they would believe him to be the man he had taken care of at the shed, the Ranger reached the adobe side wall, near the rear corner of the house. Others were visible as they crawled in.

There was a low-silled window before him, with the sash up. He put his hand on the wooden frame and vaulted inside.

Standing there for a moment, he saw the open door of the room he was in. In it were only a table and some chairs. The door led into the central hall and to his right lay the spacious living room, with a fireplace, couches, mats and other furnishings. Terence Oden was asleep, on the sofa there.

There wasn't a moment to lose. Stealthy creakings told him that his foes were seeping through the house. And into his line of vision came Cheyenne Driscoll, backed by two aides. Their bandannas were drawn up over their faces but it was easy for Hatfield to recognize Cheyenne. The man's hard eyes glittered, and in his right hand he held a knife, ten inches long, its glittering steel blade sharp and pointed. The other two men held a gunnysack, the opening stretched between their hands.

They glided past Cheyenne, to throw the bag over Oden's head, while Driscoll raised the knife to strike in case Oden awoke.

Hatfield had to shoot. He could not chance letting Oden be stabbed to the heart if there was a slip. He was in the hall just outside the main room as he raised his thumb from his Colt hammer, firing from the hip.

Driscoll uttered a shrill scream, the sound ripped from him by the blasting shock of the lead cutting his forearm. The knife flew from his hand, and he slewed around, fell to his knees and doubled up, gripping his punctured wrist.

'What the—' a voice behind Hatfield said. 'Say, who are—'

The Ranger glanced back. In action, he was as cool as ice. One of the enemy who had tiptoed through from the kitchen into the hall, had a revolver in his hand. His chin dropped as he saw the tall man against the wall.

It was a question of who fired first, and Hatfield beat him to it by the breath that spells the difference between life or death.

The reverberating explosions brought it all to a head. Shouts rose from the astonished gunnies, from Oden's waddies in the near-by bunkhouse. Hatfield jumped into the living room.

The two men with Driscoll who had been detailed to seize Oden were slow drawing their guns.

Oden jumped up, swearing, and reaching for a holstered pistol.

Cheyenne Driscoll pulled himself together with a vicious snarl. With his left hand he whipped a revolver from his belt, and swung the muzzle on the rancher. Hatfield had to stop him a second time, and he fired at Driscoll's center. Cheyenne crashed back, knocked off his feet by the stunning force of the .45 bullet. He twitched on the floor, and the appalled pair with the gunnysack dropped everything and turned to scramble ignominiously out of the windows.

Somewhere a girl began screaming at the top of her voice:

'Fa-ther! Fa-ther!'

Only breaths had elapsed since the night fight had opened up. The Ranger did not waste a move. Aware that Driscoll's killers were covering the windows and doors, he sent his next slug into the table lamp, shutting off the light.

'This way, Oden!' he called. 'Move out of there before they blast yuh!'

Guns hastily flashed from two windows. He could hear Oden moving toward him. Evidently the shrewd rancher was down on his hands and knees, out of direct line of fire from the windows.

'Here I am, Oden!' Hatfield called. 'Driscoll tried to stab yuh and I let him have it. Better stick here till yore men drive 'em off.'

'Who in tarnation blazes is it?' gasped the rancher.

'Tell yuh later. I got on to the plan to take yuh out tonight and finish yuh, so I was here, on the job.'

His cool tones, the fact that Oden knew the stranger had saved him, brought the rancher to his side. The girl's cries came nearer, and they heard her running up the hall in her bare feet.

'Lily! Here I am—I ain't hurt.'

'Dad!'

Her soft white-clad figure brushed past the tall officer and Oden took her in his arms.

'I'll make sure they're on their way, Oden,' Hatfield said.

He glided down the hall, and sought a window on the other side. Shouts, gunshots, the whinnying of horses and beat of hoofs mingled together in the yard. Driscoll's men were running as Oden's waddies surged toward the ranchhouse to fight it out.

The Ranger could follow the quick battle by ear, and as the enemy beat a hasty retreat before the aroused cowboys, he swung and reached for the 'makin's.' He needed a smoke, for he had had to refrain while awaiting the scrap.

He rolled a cigarette, licked the paper edge and sealed it. Then he struck a match, to light up. Seeing a candle on the table of the side room he was in, he touched his match to the wick, after he had started his cigarette.

As he turned to leave the room, an excited young waddy, one of Oden's crew, jumped through the doorway, a Colt leveled on him. 'Reach!' he commanded.

'All right, son, I'm reachin'. But I'm with yuh, not agin yuh.'

'We'll let the Boss call that turn,' growled the cowboy, a lean youth with pleasant eyes and a clean, tanned face. He was in bare feet, and hatless, having been roused from his sleep.

Hatfield went up the hall, under the Colt. Oden and Lily were in the living room. The danger past, the rancher struck a match and lit a lamp.

'Hey, Boss, I got a prisoner!' called the waddy.

'Fetch him here.'

Hatfield walked into the living room, nodded to the frowning Oden. Lily, with a silk wrapper thrown over her sleeping clothes now, looked so lovely that the tall Ranger stared at her in frank admiration. The excitement had brought the color to her cheeks and she was vivid even in repose, with her dark hair and long lashes.

'Pouch that gun, Dinny,' snapped Oden. 'This hombre saved my hide and all of us just now.'

The crestfallen waddy blinked, but obeyed. He turned under his employer's frown and left quickly.

Oden came direct to the point.

'Mister,' he said to Hatfield, 'I seen yuh at Luther Sherrall's. Figgered at the time that yuh might be one of his dirty killers. We knew he had gunnies hid near at hand, but we thought we could scare him by tellin' him that he was Number One in case of a scrap. Now you come in suddenlike and blast Cheyenne Driscoll and his men. I seen yuh before yuh doused the light.'

'He was standing in the hall, Father,' broke in Lily.

There was reciprocal admiration in the girl's glance as she watched the Ranger. Rugged, tall, his power obvious in the set of his stalwart body, Hatfield attracted men and women at sight.

'Yeah, Oden,' he drawled, 'I was waitin' outside when Cheyenne come along. They meant to take yuh out and drygulch yuh, and if they couldn't run yuh off, they was ordered to knife yuh.'

The lean, somber Oden was a strong man and a clever one. The gray in his crisp hair was no sign of his weakening. His wiry black mustache bristled as he heard of the enemy's plot to kill him, and his gnarled, big-knuckled hands clenched. Suddenly he slammed his fist into the palm of his other hand, and snarled.

'Luther Sherrall, of course. Cheyenne's his Number One strong-arm man.'

'Oh—oh! Water—water! Give me a drink!'

The groans came from Cheyenne Driscoll, who had not moved since going down under the Ranger's gun. There was a dark pool of blood on the oak flooring near his doubled-up form.

'Dowg me if he ain't lucky!' exclaimed Oden, stooping to investigate.

'That finisher hit him in the fancy buckle under his cartridge belt!' Hatfield said. 'See, it's twisted.' He pointed to the three-inch-square metal buckle which fastened the thick belt holding up Cheyenne's pants. 'Metal deflected it enough so the bullet was turned. But he's got a nasty slash in the side. Don't know whether yuh'd call him lucky or not, Oden.'

The gray-green eyes, watching the tortured Driscoll's face, were dark.

'Huh, yuh're right,' agreed Oden. 'From what I seen of yore gunthrowin' this evenin' no man could be called lucky who gets at the wrong end of yore Colt. Wonder how bad this sidewinder's hurt?'

'Oh, give me a slug of whiskey, give me water—anything!' begged Cheyenne, tears streaming from his eyes. 'Hays, make 'em treat me decent. Yuh're a pard of mine. Help me.'

'Yore talk ain't as salty as it was before yuh swallered lead, Cheyenne,' observed the Ranger.

He was none too pleased that Cheyenne was still alive and kicking. Such a man would never cease to be a menace until he was pushing up the daisies.

'We better tote him back to the bunkhouse where the boys can see to him,' suggested Oden. 'Enemy or not, he's hurt and we got to make him as comfortable as possible.' He raised his voice, shouting: 'Bucky—Van! Come here!'

While waiting for the waddies to appear, Oden poured a glass of water from the pitcher on the table, and gave Cheyenne a few swallows, while Hatfield smoked a quirly, arms folded. Lily Oden went to the kitchen to heat water and supply strips of clean linen to bandage the wounded foe.

Oden's cowboys picked Cheyenne up, to place him on a blanket which they would use as a stretcher. He screamed in pain at being moved, apparently weak and in a state of shock. When they took him off, to put him in a bunk and treat his wounds, the Ranger and

Oden were left together in the living room.

'Now we can talk, mister,' Oden said. 'Yore handle is Hays? That's what Cheyenne called yuh.'

'I used that name just to fool Sherrall and his boys,' explained the tall officer. 'My real handle is Jim Hatfield, and I'm from Cap'n Bill McDowell's office in Austin.'

From a secret pocket in his shirt, hidden by the bulge of his armpit, he brought the silver star on silver circle, emblem of the Texas Rangers.

'I savvy!' Oden's whistle showed his pleased surprise. 'A Ranger! Mighty glad to see yuh, Hatfield, and yuh shore give us a great sample of Ranger fightin' power. Let's have a drink and hunt up a bite to eat.'

CHAPTER EIGHT

EXPOSED

With a bottle and a cold snack between them on the kitchen table, Jim Hatfield and Oden sat down to chat. Hatfield skillfully drew out all the information the rancher possessed, concerning the projected dam, Bud Lockhart, and the trouble that had ensued since the engineer's disappearance.

'Seems pretty certain this Sherrall took over

the idea of the dam,' said the Ranger, 'and means to cash in on it. There's plenty of profit for him and his men, sellin' off the range, and then, as yuh mentioned, he can charge anything he wants for water from the dam. Yuh ain't seen Lockhart at all?'

'Not since that night of the meetin' when we decided to build the dam. I'm afraid Sherrall's men killed him, like they did Vogel.'

'I'm goin' back to Dry River—or Paradise, as Sherrall's named it,' Hatfield said, 'and stick there as long as I can. I'm expectin' to make a secret run to the dam, and see what I can find there, soon as possible. Sherrall thinks I'm a customer. Keep Cheyenne under guard, so's he can't get to Sherrall, and I'll be in touch with yuh pronto. And better put three or four waddies around yore ranch after dark, so's they can't surprise yuh agin.'

After eating and drinking, Hatfield looked in at the bunkhouse, where Cheyenne Driscoll lay on his bed of pain. They had cleansed his wounds and covered them with clean cloths, and he kept his eyes closed, his face sickly under his coat of tan.

'Reckon he won't move for a few days, anyway,' remarked Terence Oden.

Hatfield whistled up the golden sorrel, who came trotting in at his call. Oden shook hands, then watched the tall man ride down the lane to the road.

It was in the small hours when Jim Hatfield

left Goldy at the stable and started for the building where he was supposed to be sleeping. Paradise was quiet. The Ranger was surprised at this, for he had thought some of Cheyenne's gang would have returned by now and reported to Sherrall the fiasco at the Dot O. Hatfield reconnoitered, but all seemed peaceful, and he tiptoed into his room.

Jervis was snoring blissfully in his bunk. The Ranger caught the sound of another sleeper, and investigated. Another man was occupying a third bed in the customers' barracks. But there was nothing to alarm the Ranger, and he felt he must have a sleep, if only a short one, after his long exertions . . .

When he opened his eyes, the sun was shining in the side windows. Jervis and the other customer were stretching, making ready to rise. The stranger was a short, stocky fellow, and he quickly introduced himself as Ben Tate, a cowman from the Red River district, on the hunt for western range.

'Gettin' too crowded for me up there,' he told them.

The smell of frying bacon, and boiled coffee sifted through the morning air, still cool from the night. Hatfield, after his brief sleep, felt strengthened and refreshed, and ready for the meal.

As they finished their dressing, a heavy tread sounded at the front door, and a man in black frock coat, white shirt and silk bow tie, striped trousers and black shoes with elastic sides, entered the barracks. His hair needed cutting, curling dark around his thick neck. His stomach hung full, bulging out the coat. His face was weak, thought the Ranger, for his chin receded, and his cheeks were lax, the skin blemished by moles. He had a long, slender nose, which seemed to point his quarry as a bird dog might.

'Ah, gentlemen, good morning,' he greeted. 'What a beautiful day we are blessed with! As the great poet Milton puts it:

'Sweet is the breath of morn, her rising sweet,
With charm of earliest birds; pleasant the sun
When first on this delightful land he spreads
His orient beams on herb, tree, fruit and flower,
Glist'ring with dew; fragrant the fertile earth.'

'Howdy, Senator, howdy!' boomed Tate, the stocky Red River cowman, interrupting the sloppy man's oration, delivered with hand to heart and gestures. 'Yeah, the morn's smelly round here, but what gets me most of all is the breath of that fryin' bacon and coffee.'

The Senator chuckled. 'Ah, my friend Tate, you are entirely practical. Well, well, perhaps you're right.' The Senator cleared his throat. From under his coat tail he produced a flask of whisky, took a long swallow and, beaming, passed it to Tate. 'Help yourselves, boys. It cuts the acids of the night, and brings new hope to the most wilted flower.'

'Better'n dew, at that.' Tate laughed, tilting the bottle.

The Senator turned. 'Jervis, we met when I chanced upon you and, luckily for both of us, sent you here. But this tall and handsome young man I haven't had the pleasure of meeting before.' He glanced at Hatfield. 'Are you, by any chance, James Hays, sir? Counsellor Sherrall mentioned you as being one of our fortunate prospects.'

'Yes suh, that's me, Senator.'

'H'm. I am Senator Madison T. Baggett. Perhaps you have heard my modest name? Austin is my usual habitat, but the lures and beauties of Paradise have proved too much for me. Yes, it's lovely country. I am thinking of building a winter home here. Of course my career keeps me in the capital a good deal of the time, alas I love the beauties and peace of Nature, but duty calls, duty calls.'

The bottle had made the rounds and the Senator paused to take another long swig. He smacked his wet lips as he slid it back into his rear pocket.

He came toward Hatfield, holding out a pudgy hand which was none too clean. His coat collar made a dark line where it had rubbed the back of his fat-creased neck. As he looked into the Ranger's face, a puzzled light came into his eyes, and he licked his lips again.

'Uh—young man, have we met before? You

have a rather familiar look to me. Now where could it have been?'

Hatfield had seen Baggett in Austin, although he had never had any personal contact with the politico.

'Oh, shore, Senator,' he said. 'We shook hands at a vote-gettin' rally last fall. Don't you remember? In San Antonio. You made a great speech that day. I always enjoy yore speeches.'

The quick compliments took Baggett's mind off the tall man's identity. Baggett beamed, expanding under the flattery.

'Thank you, my boy, thank you. I try to hit the nail on the head, as it were.' He squeezed Hatfield's hand with a moist, warm paw.

'How about breakfast, Senator?' asked Tate.

'Let us go at once and regale ourselves. Remember, it's on the company. We offer our guests the best of everything.'

The Senator led the three customers to a restaurant at the side of the hotel, where a waitress smiled upon the big Ranger and took their order of coffee, ham and eggs, and biscuits. The warm food was welcome to Hatfield, who kept up with all but the Senator, whose appetite was prodigious.

They were on the third helping when a man came in and approached Baggett. Excusing himself, the Senator read the missive which the messenger gave him.

'Ah, yes, gentlemen,' he said. 'Counsellor

Sherrall will be delighted to see you at his office immediately.'

Baggett waddled rather than walked. His coat tails flapped about his stout legs as they walked down the street. Sherrall was at the company headquarters on the plaza, seated behind his desk. He leaned on his thick cane, nodding and smiling as they entered. They all sat down.

'Tate, glad to know you,' the attorney said. 'We've arranged to start you out at once. Jervis, you've already told me you'll take the section shown you. That leaves you, Hays. Have you made up your mind yet?'

'Just about, Counsellor,' replied Hatfield seriously. 'Reckon I'll buy in, but as I told yuh I got to wire for funds. It takes a day or two, so I'll hang around if it's all the same to you.'

'That suits me perfectly.'

Hatfield had a queer, instinctive urge to follow Tate and Jervis out, but he was left in the office with Sherrall and Senator Baggett. He had nothing to go upon, only an inner warning. There was a change in the atmosphere which his delicately attuned being detected. He shifted to get up.

'Sit still, Hays,' Sherrall said.

Instantly alert, from the corner of his eye he saw metal glinting behind the big map panel. Guns were covering him. Sherrall opened his snuff-box to take a delicate pinch and sneeze it off.

'Did you have a pleasant ride last night?' the lawyer said in a calm voice.

'Huh? What's that?' Hatfield played obtuse, hoping to gain some opportunity to save himself.

'When the Senator brought Tate in, your bunk was empty,' went on Sherrall.

Hatfield breathed more easily. If that were all, he might explain it away.

'Oh, shore,' he said. 'I couldn't sleep at first so I went out, got my hoss and took a ride. Sort of excited, I reckon, over the new range, Counsellor.'

Sherrall's heavy, somber manner did not relax. He cleared his throat, speaking evenly, softly.

'Your excitement knows no bounds. You got so excited you rode all the way out to the Dot O, shot my good friend Cheyenne Driscoll and other aides of mine, and told Oden—'

As Hatfield's eyes glowed, the softness deserted Sherrall's voice.

'Sit where you are or we'll blow you to bits!'

For a flash the Ranger considered killing Sherrall before the guns of the enemy opened up from the wall embrasures. He was sure he could get his Colt out and going before he could be finished off. But he detected a slight uncertainty in Sherrall, and Baggett was obviously mystified.

'Counsellor, what's wrong?' the Senator said. 'What has our friend Hays done? Your note simply said to bring him here.'

'When he went out last night,' explained Sherrall, 'he visited the Dot O, warned Oden against me. He killed one of my men and painfully wounded Cheyenne, Baggett. He's a spy, a range detective perhaps, whom Oden hired to bedevil us.'

At Sherrall's signal, given by hand as he spoke, armed men rushed from the back room and came up behind the Ranger. They slipped his Colts from his holsters, and swift hands patted him up and down, feeling for hidden weapons.

'Somethin' under his shirt, Counsellor,' reported a tall gunny with reddish hair and beard, and a lobster skin. 'It feels like a sheriff's star, sort of.'

'Get it. Careful he doesn't use you as a shield, Red.'

A freckled hand ripped the buttons from Hatfield's shirt, opening it from the side, and then reached in to pick the star, set on silver circle, from the inside pocket. 'Red' held it aloft, and a cold silence fell over the gathering.

CHAPTER NINE

'THEY'VE GOT CHEYENNE!'

Counsellor Sherrall broke the silence. He sniffed, licking his bluish lips.

'I've rather expected you, Ranger,' he said suavely. 'I knew Oden had sent a complaint to Austin. Of course, he lied about me.'

Senator Baggett was perturbed. He blinked rapidly several times, hemmed and hawed, his pudgy hands working. Then he puffed himself up.

'Young man,' he said importantly, 'I warn you I have great influence at the capital. I must say your acting as a spy here doesn't rate you very high in my opinion.'

'In that case,' drawled Hatfield pleasantly, 'I reckon I'm on the right track, Senator.'

Death faced the tall officer, but he showed not the slightest alarm. He sat easily in the chair, watching Luther Sherrall. His official connection with the Texas Ranger worried the Counsellor, who was turning over the development in his mind. Sherrall took another pinch of snuff.

'You've made a serious error here, Ranger,' the lawyer began. 'This is a legitimate enterprise. My standing is excellent and, as the Senator says, he can deal with you in Austin, through your superiors. Perhaps, in talking with Oden, you were deceived by his lies.'

'Perhaps, Counsellor.'

Baggett and Sherrall exchanged glances. Four men with guns, including Red, stood just out of leaping distance, covering Hatfield.

'Oden and his gang wish to rob us of our hard-won gains by taking over the Water Company. He's threatened my life and fired on us. Actually I've been thinking of requesting Ranger protection myself. There isn't much in the way of law enforcement in these distant parts. What would you say if I offered you the job of guarding the company's headquarters here? I'll pay you fifty dollars a week—a good deal more than you receive as a Ranger.'

'I'd say you can't bribe the Rangers, Counsellor,' answered Hatfield. 'You savvy that as well as I do. So does Baggett. If yuh ain't done anything wrong, yuh'll get my protection free, and yuh'll have nothin' to worry about.'

'I might say the same for you,' Sherrall said acidly. 'You're mixing in matters which don't concern you. Oden has pulled the wool over your eyes, but if you insist on fighting me, you'll have to take the consequences.'

'Rangers seldom travel alone,' observed Baggett. 'Where's your troop, my boy?'

'Closer'n yuh might think.'

Sherrall was thinking aloud, feeling for a

70

way to get hold of the imperturbable officer.

'If a Ranger committed a crime,' he said musingly, 'he'd be as liable to punishment as an ordinary citizen.'

'More so.' Hatfield nodded. 'Not many go wrong, Counsellor.'

'A few have.'

Baggett nodded vigorously as he realized what Sherrall was driving at.

'Yes, it would make it much easier in Austin, Counsellor, if this fellow did something wrong.'

'Cheyenne can testify that he killed one of our boys and seriously injured Driscoll himself.' Sherrall pursued the idea he had hit upon.

Baggett shook his head doubtfully. 'My dear Counsellor, worthy as Cheyenne appears in our estimation, unfortunately he hasn't the same high standing in other parts. As you know better than I, it's necessary to enter a court of law with clean hands and mens sibi conscia recti—a clear conscience. I, for one, would hesitate to stake my reputation on Cheyenne's testimony. Think what a clever prosecutor might bring out.'

'You're right,' agreed Sherrall. 'We must have witnesses integer vitae scelerisque purus.'

'Ah, Horace has a trenchant yet elegant manner of putting things,' gushed Baggett. 'Yes, our witnesses must be blameless of life and free from crime.'

The two were competing in an effort to impress the Ranger with their erudition, perhaps hoping to influence him. High-falutin as their talk was, at heart he knew them to be thieves and rascals, and he promised himself that he would pin them to the wall.

'We'll find the right men easily enough,'— Sherrall nodded—'and in the meantime, if it doesn't work out, there's always another way.'

A faint smile touched the Ranger's wide mouth. He sat slouched in his chair, unruffled. They were planning to buy witnesses who would swear to it that he had committed some serious crime, so that he would be helpless against them. They would keep him a prisoner, and kill him if it became necessary.

Suddenly there rose on the warm morning air the crackling of guns, and beating hoofs made the earth tremble. Raucous howls came to them, and Senator Baggett jumped nervously, thrusting a fat hand into the right-hand pocket of his coat. Evidently he carried a pistol there. Color drained from his dirty cheeks.

'Wh-what's that, Counsellor?' he gasped. 'The Rangers?'

Sherrall was on his feet, grasping his thick cane, and gliding to the front window. Cowboy whoops mingled with increasing Colt and shotgun fire. The lawyer swung about.

'Quick, Red!' he shouted. 'It's the Dot O attacking! Call your reserves out there and check 'em before they get in here.'

In the rising din a stentorian voice rose, carrying to them on the breeze. It was a voice trained to compete with roaring northers that swept the plains, and the booming of a stampeding herd. It was Terence Oden shouting at the full capacity of his powerful lungs.

'Hat-field! Hat-field! They rescued Cheyenne Driscoll! Danger! Hatfield, Danger!'

Baggett's jaw dropped and he began to shake in his boots.

'Now I place you! You're Jim Hatfield, Cap'n McDowell's star Ranger! Counsellor, this man is the most dangerous of antagonists! We dare not take any chances with him, and McDowell's incorruptible. He'll go to any lengths to help his Rangers!'

Heavy treads shook the building as gunmen ran out to do battle with the Dot O. Oden had come to warn the Ranger, but he was outnumbered by the enemy, who held positions of vantage at house corners and other spots.

Buckshot and pistol slugs shrieked in the air. A Dot O mustang went down, spilling his rider, and Terence Oden paused, leaning down to help his man mount behind him. A chunk of shot hit his cheek, and blood spurted from the rancher's leathery flesh as he fired his Colt and pressed the charge straight at

73

Sherrall's office.

Hatfield was tensed and ready to seize his chance, for no longer were guns trained on him from the wall loopholes. Only the men in the office covered him. Baggett was nearest. Red had moved to the inner door, to order out the fighters in the rear. Now, eager to take some potshots at the cowmen, Red dashed straight across the big room toward a window, and his course brought him within a yard of the seated Ranger.

Red's excited lunge drew the eyes of Sherrall and all the others just for an instant. Hatfield seized this moment to make his play.

A long leg moved out, tripping the lanky redhead, who fell heavily, sprawling on his stomach. Hatfield threw himself from his chair straight at Baggett, as Sherrall, recovering, swung his cane to cover the officer.

Steel hands gripped the Senator. Half crouched, the Ranger had Baggett for a shield, and a slim, skillful hand snatched the snub-nosed revolver from the loose pocket. Back to the wall, Hatfield had a gun cocked, and Baggett between him and Sherrall.

Baggett instantly realized his own danger.

'Don't shoot, Counsellor!' he screamed in frantic terror. 'You'll hit me! Hold your fire! I beg of you, don't shoot!'

Baggett's nerve collapsed. He was afraid of Hatfield to begin with, since he had learned his real identity. His face was chalky, and he blubbered as he screamed at Sherrall to save him.

'Back up, cuss you, Senator, or I'll blow yore back buttons through that fat stomach yuh love so much,' snarled Hatfield.

There was the open side window, only a few feet away. Baggett gingerly moved with the Ranger, taking short steps, but his knees were so weak he could hardly stand up. His eyes bulged and he kept sobbing and licking his lips, begging Sherrall not to fire.

Red had come up on his hands and knees, and was reaching for the Colt he had dropped when Hatfield tripped him. The other three gunnies were up front, where they had moved when the bottle opened in the plaza.

With the Senator as a shield, though Sherrall's teeth were bared in a snarl of fury, the Ranger put a long leg through the window opening, keeping the short-barreled revolver on the Counsellor. Either because Sherrall needed Baggett in his ambitious schemes or because he knew that the first bullet from the pistol would be aimed his way, the lawyer did not open up.

With a quick movement, Hatfield threw himself bodily outside, and pushed from under Sherrall's window.

A quick glance up the passage to the street showed that as Sherrall's gunnies concentrated their lead, the Dot O had been stopped. They had been forced to rereat from certain death.

A few feet down the way, in the wall opposite the office, was a closed window leading into the next building, and Hatfield tapped the glass with the gun barrel, stabbing it in. He dived through, landing on a wooden floor in the side room evidently used as a storage space for the hardware store up front.

Sherrall was yelling frantically, hoping to check the bold escape dash made by the Ranger.

'Shoot him down! Get that man!'

CHAPTER TEN

THE CAPTIVE

Bud Lockhart wearily dragged his bruised bare feet up the rocky path to the big mixing troughs in which workers were stirring cement and sand together. At the other end of the path more laborers were busy filling barrows with the gray stuff and trundling them to the molds forming the dam breast.

They had taken away Lockhart's shoes, as a precaution against attempted escape. He wore an old outfit which had been discarded by Enrique Pereda, the driving Mexican overseer whom Lockhart had grown to loathe with a fury which sometimes threatened to consume him. Ragged brown pants, an old shirt and a steeple sombrero made up Lockhart's costume.

Face burned by sun and wind, drawn from sickness, he was hardly recognizable as the smiling, stalwart engineer who had addressed the Dry River Ranchers. He was ill from a fever brought on by exposure, and aggravated by the deadly worry which gnawed at his young mind.

It was a beautiful day but Lockhart had no appreciation of Nature's charm at the moment. He was in no mood to enjoy such pleasures.

'Senor Ingenier, come check zees,' called Pereda, who was standing on a high point watching the operations.

The handsome vaquero always maintained that condescending, insufferable air of superiority, his speech polite, but with a sneer in his dark eyes as he regarded Lockhart. The smile seldom left Enrique's lips, and the knife, pistol and thick-butted black whip were with him always.

Grudgingly, Lockhart had to admit that Pereda was unusually intelligent. He had evidently had some experience at construction work, also, and was first class at supervising workers. They all feared him, and his whip and other weapons.

Lockhart stooped, to feel the cement.
'It's all right, Enrique.'
'Bueno. Soon we have her feeled up, si.'

A husky Irishman paused to wipe the sweat from his brow with a red bandanna he whisked from his hip pocket.

'Hey, Enrique!' he called. 'You hear from the Office yet? We want our money.'

'Work,' ordered Pereda. 'You weel get eet, pronto. But you mus' work, Murphee.'

Lockhart was aware that the company was behind in the laborers' wages. It had been two weeks since the men had received any money, and they were growing discontented. The food was poor, too, tasteless and ill-cooked—that is, the food served Lockhart and the workers. The guards and Pereda fared well enough.

Many of the Irish and Mexican workmen would have quit, but they had no transportation, and they feared Pereda's vengeance. Worn out at the end of the hard day, they ate and slept. In not too long a time they would finish the earth dam and be free to leave.

As for Bud Lockhart, he was giving of his trained skill as an engineer, making the dam as good a piece of construction as possible. He had a will to live, to gain revenge on Sherrall, and help Terence Oden and the decent ranchers of the vicinity regain their property.

Luther Sherrall had promised that he would be set free once the dam was finished, but Lockhart knew, instinctively, that actually they planned to kill him when his usefulness had passed. He was far too dangerous a witness against them all to be allowed to live. Yet he dragged on, hoping that some opportunity to escape might come.

They had had his blue-prints and plans, since his baggage had been brought along when Enrique Pereda had made him a captive that night at Paradise. The dam construction was so simple that even had they killed Lockhart they could have gone ahead and completed it. Yet there were details which he, as a trained engineer, could assist and advise on, so they kept him on hand.

The work had proceeded at driving speed. Teams of oxen and horses had scooped the earth and crushed rock into the narrow gap where the valley shoulders converged. Timber for the forms had been cut by a portable sawmill from adjacent stands of pine. Cement and metal strips to reinforce it had been brought in by wagon.

Once the pouring of the cement was done, and the stuff hardened somewhat, the spillway gate would be closed and the river would begin slowly rising behind its artificial barrier.

Below the site of the dam, the camp stood—rough shacks and canvas shelters for the workers and their overseers, the cook shed, with stacks of cut wood and outdoor oven and spits, and piles of pipe, bags of cement, tools and other needed gear. Up the slope, among the trees on the west, stood a small log stockade in which they placed Lockhart at night for safe-keeping, under alert guard. Whenever visitors came, their approach warned of by sentries on the trails, Lockhart was hustled there and hidden.

There had been some excitement just before dawn that day. The restless, feverish engineer, tossing in the warm nights, had been aware of it. He had heard shouts, the sounds of saddling up at the corral in the woods where the guards kept their horses ready, not far from the stockade. That corral was under guard day and night, just as the stockade was.

The men had ridden out, to return after breakfast. Pereda had gone along, and the Mexican overseer had slept until 4 P.M. that afternoon to make up for lost rest.

A call came from below, past the camp, and Enrique turned to watch a sentry's signaling.

'Come, Senor Ingenier,' he ordered, 'we go down.'

Lockhart shrugged, and preceded the lithe Mexican knifeman. A body of riders appeared, coming from the direction of the road to Dry River—or Paradise, as it had been rechristened. One of them was Luther Sherrall, on a black mustang, and the rest were guards, led by a red-haired gunny whom Lockhart had seen before.

When Enrique and Bud Lockhart reached the tents and shacks, Sherrall had dismounted and was leaning on his thick cane. He looked disturbed, and his lax lower lip trembled with self-pity as he turned to Pereda.

'I've had a bad time of it, Enrique,' said the counsellor, unhappily. 'I needed you and Cheyenne with me. Red's a good boy, but he's inexperienced and young. A Texas Ranger named Jim Hatfield has been spying on us. He's made me a great deal of trouble.'

'Hey!' Pereda jumped, and his white teeth shone. 'I do not like zees Texas Rang-aire.' He fondled the whip butt in his brown hands. 'You keel?'

Sherrall shook his head. For a moment, Lockhart's heart leaped, as he heard there was a Ranger in the vicinity. He hoped that perhaps rescue might be at hand, but as the lawyer went on he realized the officer was alone and evidently up against overwhelming odds.

'He escaped, but I've got men hunting him. We'll get him sooner or later. He managed to call his horse—a golden sorrel which comes to him when he whistles. It's a serious matter, though, so I came to warn you. This Ranger posed as a rancher, said his name was Hays. He came out here with Cheyenne. They stopped here, didn't they?'

'Si, si. I remem-baire! Beeg hombre, black hair, tough look in hees eyes. He try to get to stockade where I hav' Lockhart.'

'That's the man. Shoot him on sight, Enrique. And don't let Lockhart get loose, whatever you do.'

'He weel not es-cape.' Pereda grinned at the engineer.

'You did a beautiful job at the Dot O, rescuin' Cheyenne last night,' complimented Sherrall. 'I wish all my men came up to your specifications, Enrique.'

'Was not easy, Senor Counsellor. Cheyenne's vaqueros rode here at once, to tell me, so I hurr-ee to be in time. Zey were not set, not expecting me, but still it was hard.'

'How's Cheyenne?'

Enrique shrugged. 'So-so. He suffaire mucho. All he weesh ees to keel zat hombre Hays—zat Rang-aire.'

Murphy, the big Irishman, had trailed down, and now he came up to Sherrall.

'Now lookit here, Sherrall,' he said in a loud voice, 'I told Pereda we fellers want our money. You owe us two weeks, and there's another due Sattiday.'

Sherrall frowned with impatience. 'You'll get it, Murphy. I've promised it. It's a matter of transferrin' funds from another state to another, that's all.'

'Yeah. And last week the fellers carryin' the cash out here were held up by bandits and robbed!' sneered Murphy. Evidently he had been chosen as spokesman by the other workers.

Sherrall flushed. 'You'll be paid,' he repeated. 'In the meantime, go about your work. The dam must be finished.'

'We've decided not to work no more till we get our pay, or some of it, anyways,' insisted Murphy angrily.

Pereda's lash flicked out. The leaded tip curled about Murphy's heavy thigh, stinging his flesh. The Irishman jumped and swore.

'I'll get you for that, Enrique!' he snarled.

But he broke off, aware of Enrique's temper and weapons. He moved away, scowling back at them, and hurried to rejoin the laborers. A knot of them congregated about him, to hear his report.

Armed guards were set at strategic points about the camp. Enrique signaled them, and several, shotguns in the crooks of their arms, strolled toward the dam.

'Hey, there, Counsellor!' The voice that spoke was Cheyenne Driscoll's. He was lying wounded in a near-by tent, which had its sides rolled up. He had been dozing, but had awakened and seen his chief.

'I'll be with you in a jiffy,' called Sherrall. To Pereda he said, with a quick glance at Lockhart, 'How much longer will you need our engineer friend?'

'I do not need heem any long-aire. Dam, she ees near done.'

'Good. Baggett's gone to see what he can do in Austin about that cursed Ranger. He has good connections. Come over here, I want to speak to Cheyenne, and to you as well.'

Enrique pointed with his whip butt at

Lockhart.

'Watch that man,' Sherrall said to Red. 'Don't let him get away.'

The Mexican and Sherrall went over to the tent. Driscoll lay on a pad on the ground, and they squatted to converse with him, for his wounds kept him down. The dejected Lockhart sat down on a flat rock to wait.

He could not hear what the three in the tent were saying, but now and then they would look his way, then turn back to their discussion. He felt weak, helpless. He was sick, and saw no chance of escaping.

'They're going to kill me.'

The conviction swept over him. That was what they had decided. The arrival of the Texas Ranger had hastened his fate, although Sherrall had meant all along to finish him.

Wildly fighting to maintain outward calm, Lockhart looked about, wondering how to start at getting away. His feet were bare and in the hills they would soon be cut to ribbons on sharp rocks and gravel. He had no weapons, no horse.

Up to this point he had had hope to sustain him, a hope that as long as they needed his skill and advice they would not destroy him. Now that was gone.

It was a difficult struggle for him to regain his self-control, face his fate with fortitude. Sickening depression was upon his soul. He thought of Lily Oden, of his parents in the

East. Life had been a joy to him, with his career, and meeting Lily had given it a new meaning. He was trapped, however—alive, but condemned, and he had done nothing wrong.

His heart pounded, he felt a sickness in the pit of his stomach, and he breathed swiftly. Sweat dampened the palms of his hands. A thousand little needles seemed to be pricking the flesh of his arms and legs. He wanted to cry out, to get up and run. It was fear, the fear which every man must feel when death is upon him.

He fought, panting for breath. His vision was blurred with dark streaks.

When he realized that his nails had dug deep into the palms of his hands, he was beginning to recover from the blind panic which had overwhelmed him. He drew in a deep breath and set his jaw. He would die like a man.

After a time, Pereda left the tent and came to him. The Mexican's voice was as soft as a kitten's fur and his smile oily.

'Come Senor Ingenier. You mus' be tired. I tak' you back to bed.'

CHAPTER ELEVEN

ESCAPE!

Lockhart held his head high and his step was steady as he trudged up the slope to the stockade. Pereda politely opened the wooden gate, grinning as the engineer entered. Nearby stood an armed sentry, on guard.

'I may see you later,' remarked the Mexican.

The stockade in the woods was about twenty feet by twenty, constructed of thick pine limbs sunk into the earth. It was fifteen feet high, with the top ends sharpened and two lengths of barbed wire stretched about the square over the palisades. Inside, the ground was carpeted with pine needles.

Lockhart had two dirty blankets they had given him. His food was usually brought in the same tin dish, and he was not allowed matches or tobacco, or a knife, anything which he might use in an attempt to escape. He had some harmless possessions such as papers and underclothes.

When the padlock had been snapped outside, Lockhart began restlessly pacing up and down. It was hard to sit still. He had a reprieve, if only for a few hours. Perhaps they meant to wait until dark before they killed him.

Racking his brains for some slight hope, some method of getting out, he found none. He might, at risk of tearing his flesh seriously on the barbs, have pulled himself up over the top of the pen. But there were guards at both ends of the stockade, two during the day, four at night. They remained alert, too. And the horse corral was only a hundred yards away, with more of Pereda's gunmen there.

There was the red of sunset in the sky. The night was coming. Lockhart sat down for the sickness that gripped him made him tire easily.

He started when he heard someone at the lock of the gate an hour later. But it was only a cook shoving in his tin plate of supper with a cup of water.

He tried to eat but had little appetite, and the food stuck in his throat. Then night fell over the wilderness. Insects and birds, free in their world, piped about the woods. Now and then Bud Lockhart caught the muffled tread of one of the sentries, or a horse would whinny at the corral.

The camp below was quiet. The workers slept in open-sided barracks, roofed by slabs of pine. Usually they made some noise together, before going to sleep, but this evening Lockhart did not hear their distant voices.

He lay down on his blanket, putting his head on his arm, curled up against the dampening of the air as the dew fell . . .

Starting up from a feverish doze, he heard

shouting in the main camp. It was an angry sound such as a hive of disturbed bees might make.

A shotgun belched, and a terrible screech of pain following the explosion.

'Zees way, boys!' he heard Pereda's voice calling over the din. 'Geeve zem peegs what they ask for!'

Lockhart jumped up, his ears alert, listening. There was a terrific hubbub in the camp.

'Hey, Pereda, what goes on down there?' bellowed one of the stockade sentries. His voice echoed in the hills but evidently Enrique was too busy to answer, or else he had not heard the call.

Lockhart went to a peep-hole he had found, a crack where the edges of the palisades did not overlap, and peeked out. He could see the yellow lanterns in camp, and several dark figures ran past the beams, between him and the lights.

The gate sentry was standing several yards down the path, a black figure, faced toward the camp.

Curses, screams, with a couple more gunshots.

'They revolted!' Lockhart concluded, deciding that the exploited workmen, egged on by Murphy, had sought to take over. He hoped they would succeed. If they did, he would be freed.

But his heart fell as the tumult began to die down. The sounds abated, as Pereda regained control.

Lockhart was about to return to his blankets when he sighted a long tongue of red flame rising at the left of the camp. It was close to a wooden shed which, Lockhart knew, contained the blasting powder used in construction of the dam. The wind blew toward him, up the slope. It brought the smell of oil and wood mingling together in a conflagration, and as the ruby light of the swift-burning fire took hold of the camp clearing, he was able to see the tents and the running figures.

'Fire! Fire!'

That call was always exciting, and drew every man's fearful attention. With terrifying speed, flames licked the sides of the dry shack. The smoke began to drift in great, dark puffs, and cut off the engineer's view.

The men were hurrying to fight the fire with water from the stream.

The red glow reached into the sky. The engineer could see it as intermittent clouds of smoke parted, rolling up the hill into the woods. The smoke came straight toward the stockade, and a sentry outside it coughed, and swore.

'What's up, Mac?' called Lockhart.

'Fire down there,' growled the guard, turning toward him. 'Looks like it's right in the powder shed.'

Something shadowy sprang from the dark side of the stockade. The astonished Lockhart saw Mac, the sentinel, disappear from sight, falling back as he went. There was a dull thud, and after a minute the engineer heard someone at the gate.

The nails holding the padlock hasp were being pried out, and the gate opened.

Lockhart, turned that way, stood frozen in his tracks. He thought for a moment that Pereda had come to kill him.

'Prisoner!' a voice said in an urgent whisper. 'What's yore handle? I am a friend.'

'I'm Bud Lockhart. Who are you?'

'I thought I had it right! C'mon, now. We'll palaver later. Got to run for it while they're busy with the fire.'

'The guards—'

'I've laid out two at this end. The other pair are down the slope, watching the fire instead of you.'

A steady, strong hand seized the engineer's wrist, led him worming through the gate.

Bud Lockhart could not know it—then—but Jim Hatfield was calling on the last reserves of his great physical endurance in his attempt to help Sherrall's prisoner.

A sense of urgency drove Hatfield, heightened by the narrow escape he had had at Sherrall's office in Paradise. The lawyer was a dangerous antagonist, had proved it. Oden, who had known in what peril Cheyenne

90

Driscoll's rescue placed the Ranger, had struck instantly, and while he had failed to drive through to the actual goal, the diversion had given Hatfield the slight chance needed in which to get away.

Tricky, always thinking two jumps ahead of his foes, Hatfield had whistled up the golden sorrel, and his swift horse, reaching him after a game of hide-and-seek among the town buildings, had carried him away from town, circling to the northeast until from a crest of rolling land he had spied the Dot O men retreating before Sherrall's gunmen.

Some of the latter had mounted and chased the cowboys. Oden had lost one man and several had been hit by flying lead.

But in the open the cowmen, though outnumbered, more than held their own, and the counsellor's hirelings dared not harass the infuriated Dot O too closely. When the renegades had turned back to town after a short chase, Hatfield had angled down. Oden had greeted him with profane joy, furnished him with new six-shooters and a saddle for Goldy, since there had been no time for the Ranger to pick up his gear.

Oden had begged him to go to the ranch but Hatfield had felt he must lose no time if he hoped to win over Sherrall. He must have a secret look at the enemy's stronghold near the dam, seek to discover their dispositions. Recalling how he had been blocked from visiting that stockade in the woods above the camp, when he had been posing as a land buyer, he had been determined to check up.

After riding with Oden until the roads forked, he had borrowed a spare horse to lead, a belt of ammunition for the pistols, and a pair of field-glasses which the rancher carried in his saddle-bags. With some hardtack and a couple of canteens of water, he felt equipped for his task.

Promising Oden he would make the Dot O his next stop, after seeing to the foe's camp, he had taken to the mesquite and cut across country toward his objective, aware of the sentries who lurked on the trails near the dam.

He had hidden Goldy a mile off, and crept closer and closer until, from a height, he had been able to study the camp through the field-glasses. Through the afternoon hours he had observed the work, had seen Pereda, and Lockhart in his Mexican getup. He had noted Sherrall's arrival later in the day, had seen the workmen getting together and noticed Pereda's lashing of Murphy with the whip.

'That feller don't move like a Mexican,' he had decided, studying Lockhart's figure, and he had kept the glasses focused on Lockhart until Pereda had escorted him to the stockade and locked him in. Immediately, Hatfield had decided to contact the captive.

Yet a diversion had been necessary. The camp was swarming with enemies, with sentinels at every strategic point. After dark fell he had been enabled to draw in close, until he could hear their voices. Then had come the revolt of the workmen, and Hatfield had seized upon it as his chance to rescue the prisoner, as Pereda and his men rushed to check the trouble.

Now, Colt in his right hand, leading the weakened Lockhart with his left, the Ranger snaked through the woods toward where he had hidden the horses. Behind them glowed the rising fire, reddening the sky. Smoke drifted after them on the wind.

Lockhart coughed, stumbled, and nearly went down.

'Keep quiet, Lockhart,' urged Hatfield. 'We ain't out of it yet. There's a couple of men between us and a getaway.'

'I'm sorry!' gasped the engineer. 'I've got fever and I'm mighty weak.'

'Halt! Who's that!'

The demand came from a black thicket. Hatfield had been aware of a sentry post in that direction, but had thought it was farther out. No doubt the sentries were coming in to find what was wrong at camp, and they could see the Ranger and Lockhart against the ruby glow.

As he opened fire, throwing lead from his Colt into the thicket, the Ranger fell away, jerking Lockhart down. Bullets whirled over them, but there was a cry of pain from the thicket, and as Hatfield began to run, a steel grip on Lockhart's wrist, there was no more opposition.

'Enrique—Enrique!' a man in the brush was screaming, 'Help—escape! Enrique!'

CHAPTER TWELVE

ATTACK

Not far from the stockade in which Lockhart spent so many unhappy hours, some of Pereda's guards were at the horse corral. The crackling shots, the cries of their comrade, reached their ears.

Shouts told the Ranger that several were coming in answer to the yells of the fellow he had winged in the thicket. He veered to the right, to put distance between them and himself and Lockhart, hurrying to reach the horses.

Both were gasping for wind. Lockhart was in distress but fighting to stay on his feet. It was dark among the trees. There was a slice of moon but it only accentuated the shadows in the bush.

Glancing back, sweated hand gripping his Colt, the Ranger saw from below a sudden brilliant upheaval and for a few instants yellowish-red light showed their surroundings. Sparks and flaming brands flickered in the sky over the enemy's installments, springing from the central explosion in the flames.

'Powder shack went up!' exclaimed Hatfield, puffing after the long exertion.

The muffled booming echoed in the hills, drowning out all other sounds. For a time they could hear only the pounding in their ears, ringing from the heavy noise. Lockhart's breath rasped through his throat and lungs, and his heart raced madly.

'Here we are! We've made it!' encouraged the Ranger.

Two horses stood in a patch of evergreens. The Ranger boosted Lockhart onto the back of a dark gelding, borrowed from Oden and carrying the Dot O brand. He mounted Goldy.

'Hold on to the saddle-horn, Lockhart,' he said. 'We got to move.'

He led the Dot O mustang by a short rope. Lockhart, his teeth rattling with the horse's uneven gait, rode with head down, gripping the saddle prong. The going was rough, but the sorrel picked a way at good speed. Behind them the red glow over the enemy camp was diminishing.

Hatfield bore north from the site of the dam, choosing the easiest routes, until he was able to drop into the river valley and reach the stream. There they paused for a quick drink, and to dash water on their burning faces, then moved up the gentle slope eastward to reach the rolling country between them and the Dot O.

The Ranger set his course by the stars and the moon gave light enough to pick the road. He had eluded the enemy for the time being in the night, and had a good start. He pushed steadily on.

'Halt! Reach!'

That was Oden's gate sentinel, challenging them as they turned off the road into the lane leading to the house.

'It's Jim Hatfield—and Bud Lockhart!'

'Let's see yuh. Dog me if it ain't! Lockhart! Where in tarnation yuh been?' The cowboy was amazed. 'Ain't seen yuh since that night in town. Thought yuh was dead!'

'I—I'm still alive, I reckon,' said Lockhart faintly, essaying a jest.

'Sing out, Ranger,' warned the waddy. 'There's plenty of the boys out on guard now. Mr. Oden's waitin' up for yuh.'

'Bueno.'

Terence Oden hurried out on the veranda to seize the hands of the new arrivals. He pumped the Ranger's arm, swearing in his joy.

'Can't believe it—and yuh got Lockhart! My boy, where yuh been?'

'A prisoner,' replied Lockhart.

His voice was weaker, and he was unsteady on his feet. Oden helped him to a chair. 'Sherrall had Pereda hold me at the dam,' the engineer continued. 'Forced me to work for them and direct operations. They captured me that night after the meeting, when I spoke to you ranchers. I made a good job of the dam, because I hoped I might escape and help you settle with Sherrall, so you could get control of the water. But they were about to kill me, to cover themselves. Hatfield snatched me from them in the nick of time. You see, Sherrall killed Hans Vogel.'

'Say that again!' drawled the Ranger.

'Sherrall shot down Vogel in cold blood at his office. I was an eyewitness to it all. It was out-and-out murder.'

Lockhart's burning eyes fixed the Ranger's gray-green gaze as he described the scene at Sherrall's when Vogel had died.

'Yuh're worth yore weight in gold, Lockhart, if only for the reason yuh can convict Sherrall of that killin',' Hatfield said. 'I'm surprised he didn't have yuh done in long ago.'

'He needed me. There were technical matters that only a trained hydraulic engineer could handle. I planned the construction, had it roughed out and translated it for them.'

'I savvy Sherrall was too shore of hisself. Figgered he'd use yuh up before he killed yuh. That was his big mistake.'

'He'd have succeeded if it hadn't been for you, Hatfield,' declared Lockhart. 'They were on the point of finishing me when you appeared.'

'This is desperate business, Oden,' said Hatfield gravely. 'Sherrall will be wrecked if he lets Lockhart stroll around loose for long!

He'll have to attack, for he can't take Lockhart's escape lyin' down. Pereda and the gang'll strike pronto, the way they done when they rescued Cheyenne Driscoll.'

Oden flushed.

'I'm still kickin' myself for that, Ranger!' he mumbled.

'What happened?' inquired Lockhart.

'Hatfield learned Driscoll and some of his boys meant to kill me,' the rancher explained. 'Hatfield busted it up, and we drove 'em off in the night. Instead of headin' back to town, some of 'em rushed over to the dam and told Pereda. He brought a bunch of riders here, hit us hard. They beat off my guards at the bunkhouse and dogged if they didn't tote off Cheyenne! Driscoll told Pereda about Hatfield, who was posin' with Sherrall as a land buyer. Pereda sent Sherrall word, and it near finished Hatfield.'

'Forget it, Oden. You couldn't help it.' Hatfield shrugged. 'What we got to think of now is protectin' Lockhart and you from the attack that's shapin' up. Yuh need organization here. Yore rancher friends'll have to throw in all together and fight agin Sherrall.'

Oden nodded vigorously. 'They'd all agreed to that, Hatfield. Trouble is, every man's busy with his own affairs, till it's too late.' He smacked a fist into his other hand.

Hatfield knew that. It was part of human

nature. Men had work to do. They had to eat, sleep, make love. It was hard to rouse them against evil until they were actually victims themselves. And while Sherrall had taken over the water business, he had attacked only Oden and a few of the more vigorous cowmen who had bucked him.

'How many fighters yuh got on hand?' asked the Ranger.

'Twelve all in one piece. There's two wounded in the bunkhouse, and a couple more walkin' around with flesh scratches. We got cut up mighty bad in town.'

'Huh. Pereda can muster a lot more'n that. How about yore neighbors? Who's nearest?'

'Ed Baxter, the Bar B.'

'How big's his spread?'

'Well, say a fourth the size of the Dot O. Usually he hires ten men or so. It lies six miles cast of here.'

'Send a man over there and ask Baxter to rouse as many folks as he can and hustle here. It's a matter of life and death, to them as well as to you. Yore pard'll answer such a call. I believe Sherrall'll hit us before daybreak. He's at the camp and when he finds Lockhart gone he'll go loco.'

Oden hurried to carry out his orders.

'Got to rouse all these folks,' mused Hatfield, 'so's they can carry the fight to Sherrall. Have to check him before he does any more damage.'

'Bud!'

Lily Oden hurried from the hall into the main room, smiling her welcome. Lockhart rose, turning to her.

'Lily! It's really you!'

She took his outstretched hand and they stood looking at one another. Hatfield moved toward the door. He wanted to take care of Goldy, and then, if he had time, snatch a nap before the coming battle he was sure was shaping up.

'I'm so glad, Bud!' he heard Lily saying. 'I was afraid they'd killed you!'

'They meant to, Lily,' Lockhart told her. 'I was held a prisoner, or I'd have been here before, to see you. I've been sick, and they forced me to work for them, under the gun. All I thought about was you.'

When the Ranger glanced back, she was in Lockhart's arms. The two were oblivious to everything save one another.

Hatfield went on out and rubbed down the sorrel, caring for him with consummate skill. Then he checked Oden's defense dispositions and, finding some weak spots, bolstered them here and there. After a bite in the kitchen, he lay down and was quickly asleep . . .

He awoke with a start, fully alert. He felt refreshed and knew he had slept a few hours. A shout had awakened him.

'Here they come!'

The enemy was upon the Dot O.

The shout had come from a mounted sentry posted well out from the buildings. The Ranger sprang from his couch, and buckled on his gun-belts.

He hurried to the big front room, where Oden and several waddies were watching from windows. They were armed with shotguns, rifles and pistols, and belts of ammunition for the weapons lay at hand. Oden was peeking at the road, from the side of a window.

'Big bunch of 'em headin' in, Ranger,' announced the rancher. 'Three of Baxter's boys pulled in while yuh was sleepin'. Baxter sent me word he'd hustled to fetch more help from our neighbors. It's near five o'clock.'

A gunshot crackled on the cool morning air. The sun was not yet up but there was a red streak in the eastern sky.

'Spread out, hombres! Circle zem!' Enrique Pereda's voice gave the commands.

The ranger squatted to peek—from the other side of the window, near Oden. On the approaches to the house he saw riders circling, a line running around both wings to cast a noose about them. Oden's outriders had been driven in, had dismounted and disposed themselves at vantage points in the bunkhouse, barn or house.

There was the feeling of tense excitement which precedes a battle. All men experienced it. Hatfield, a veteran at such work, was cool of head and steady of hand but he, too, sensed it.

CHAPTER THIRTEEN

THE COUNSELLOR'S FURY

Realizing that surprise was impossible because of the alertness of the guards, the enemy pulled up just out of easy pistol range.

'Oden!' a heavy voice called. 'Terence Oden. I want a word with you.'

'That's Sherrall,' said Hatfield to the rancher. 'He's back among the gang with Pereda. See what the old buzzard has to say.'

'What yuh want, Counsellor?' demanded Oden in his stentorian tones.

'Deliver Lockhart to us, Oden.'

'What makes yuh think he's here?' parried Oden.

'It's no use to lie to us,' answered Sherrall. 'Ye know you kidnapped him from our stockade last night and brought him here. At dawn we picked up the tracks of two horses leading to this point. He's hidden in there.'

It had taken them time to follow the sign. Night trailing was extremely slow and arduous, but as soon as the light had come they had been able to check up and move faster.

'I ain't sayin' Lockhart's here, but if he was I wouldn't turn him over to a killer like you, Sherrall!' shouted Oden.

Their raised voices, harshened by anger,

echoed in the morning air.

'You'll find yourself in hot water, Oden!' flared the Counsellor. 'Lockhart killed an innocent workman, Mike Murphy, at our camp before he ran off. You've got to surrender him. The law wants him to answer for his crime. I'll guarantee that he gets a fair trial.'

Oden's raucous laughter boomed in the rosy dawn light.

'Tell him yuh'll surrender Lockhart to the nearest Texas Ranger,' prompted Hatfield.

This grim jest tickled the rancher, and he retailed it to Sherrall, whose reply was a bellow of rage.

'Is Hatfield in there?' he cried. They could see him among his crew—Pereda's heavily armed guards from the dam camp, and several gunnies who had brought the Counsellor out from Paradise. 'You tell that Ranger he can't get away with this! He'll answer for what he's done. Even a Ranger can't flout the law of Texas. There are higher authorities, and I'll see to it he's punished.'

The enemy bristled with guns, carbines and Colts. They had twice the number of men on hand that Oden could yet muster.

'Go on back where yuh came from, Sherrall!' called Oden. 'Get off my range. You're the man who'll answer to the law.'

Sherrall turned, nodded to Enrique.

'Take zem!' shrieked the Mexican.

Sherrall hurriedly pulled back, to shelter

himself behind some big cottonwoods growing outside the fence. The gunmen, faces set and guns rising, started determinedly for the ranchhouse. Their weapons opened up, and lead shrieked through the window openings, or plugged into the walls.

Howls split the ears, war cries, as they whooped it up, riding faster, zigzagging as they attacked.

It was a vicious thrust. Pereda was a shrewd field commander, and the Counsellor left the actual generalship up to the Mexican. Beating hoofs threw up the dust as the yelling killers charged, evidently concentrating on the front of the ranchhouse.

'Let 'em have it!' growled Hatfield. 'They've asked for it.'

He sent a bullet Sherrall's way, but the Counsellor was taking care of his own hide. It missed him by inches, then he was safe behind a thick-boled tree. Pereda was an elusive target, too. He kept moving, and well back, urging his men to the fight, and keeping an eye on the battle's progress.

Oden and his waddies were shooting, with the Ranger. Bud Lockhart, borrowing a shotgun, crouched at a side window to help defend the Dot O.

It was worth a man's life to show himself at a window for more than a breath, for Pereda had sharpshooters with rifles sitting back from the building, taking potshots each time a defender bobbed up. Powder smoke mingled with the raised dust and in this screen the swift-moving killers maneuvered.

The din increased, the cursing yells of fighting men, the banging of the guns, the heavy tread of the mustangs. A horse, hit by a bullet, began screaming, adding to the cacophony.

Two of Pereda's men had been thrown as their animals went down. The fire from the windows as the defenders bobbed up to shoot blasted the charging lines. The riders slowed, whirled, and rode off to the sides, the first run broken.

The Ranger Colts were shrewd, picking out the best targets to shake the enemy. Then a Dot O waddy swore and gripped his right shoulder that had been punctured by a slug.

The enemy kept yelling at the top of their lungs. They fired even when there was no visible target. Again the broken lines of horsemen whirled past the line of front windows, shooting in, forcing the defenders down.

'Pereda's smarter than this,' mused the Ranger, peeking from the corner of a window.

A bullet, one of many aimed that way, cut a chunk from his Stetson crown. He turned, suddenly aware of shouts at the rear. A Dot O cowboy dashed through the hall.

Now Hatfield could hear what he was saying. His calls had been drowned out in the racket raised up front by Pereda's bunch there.

'Hustle!' gasped the waddy, as Hatfield siezed his arm and bent his ear to catch his words. 'There's a bunch rushed the kitchen door from the tool shed, and they're inside already!'

He was pinked, dark blood trickling from a nick in his scalp. The Ranger saw Pereda's strategy then. The Mexican had attracted them, held the bulk of the Dot O up front, while his picked crew had come in the back.

Leaving Oden to handle the situation in front, Hatfield took a half dozen men and hustled through the hall. Lily Oden was waiting there, ready to help when she could. He winked at her and smiled as he passed, to reassure her, for she looked drawn with anxiety.

The foe had occupied the large kitchen. Oden's waddies were trying to block them, from a side room commanding the hall, but more and more of the gunnies were dashing up, dismounting, and running inside.

Bullets greeted the tall Ranger. The gunnies were firing into the hall, trying to dislodge the three Dot O fighters who kept them from advancing to the living room and catching Oden in the rear.

Ranger Colts began belching stinging lead. Hatfield's reinforcements, whooping it up, charged through. Splinters flew from a heavy wooden table the killers had upended to use as cover. At close range, the bullets tore through it, and Pereda's men hastily ducked back.

Driving them to the walls, Hatfield leaped in. His pistols roared, raking them, and their nerve broke. They dived out the open windows, scrambling for safety, and those outside, seeing their twisted, scared faces, drew back.

'Whew!' gasped a Dot O waddy, mopping the sweat from his burning face. 'That was close!'

But it was the end of the battle. The killers withdrew to a safer distance, kept up a fire, yelling threats and challenges at the defenders. They had been chewed up badly, and had failed to take the ranch.

Hatfield went back to the living room. He watched the enemy as they gathered in a knot around Pereda and Sherrall. After a time the Counsellor and his bodyguard rode away, taking the road south toward Paradise, but Pereda remained with most of his followers, throwing a ring of death around the Dot O.

'Reckon Sherrall's gone to scrape up more gunnies, Oden,' decided Hatfield. 'But by the time they fetch 'em, we'll have reinforcements too. Yore friends should be along soon.'

The tension eased off. Men began to jest, describing their individual experiences in the fight which had taken place, teasing their comrades. Lily, who was her father's housekeeper since the death of her mother five years previously, began to prepare a hearty breakfast for the hungry men, directing the fat Mexican woman who acted as chief cook. The men washed up, and from a safe distance the gunman kept an eye on them.

'Goin' to try and hold us in,' said the Ranger to Oden. 'Sherrall's wild, like I said. Lockhart's escape'll wreck him.'

'We'll nail his cussed hide to the wall yet,' growled Oden, smacking his fist into his open hand in his familiar gesture.

The sun was well up, and the range warming with its yellow rays, when they heard some shots eastward of the buildings. After a time, a knot of men, fifteen in number, came galloping through. Baxter, Oden's neighbor, led them. He had collected them from other ranches and had come to the Dot O's assistance.

The Ranger was planning his next move. He knew he must crush Luther Sherrall before the range would be safe for the decent citizens of Dry River. But the Counsellor was still powerful, held many aces.

Hatfield needed a real sleep. He had had but snatches since coming to Dry River. The few hours he had enjoyed the night before had given him the strength to fight at full tilt in the battle, but he craved more. The hot meal of coffee, meat and bread, served by Lily Oden, made him comfortably full and drowsy. After making sure the sentinels were posted and the enemy still lying well out from the ranch, he turned in.

*   *   *

In the afternoon when he was awakened, it was to discover that a couple of Pereda's followers were escorting a third man in from the road. They were coming under a flag of truce, a white cloth waved on a stick.

They halted out from the stoop.

'What yuh want, cuss yuh?' Oden called.

The third man pushed his horse forward. He held a yellow envelope in one hand.

'Say, I got a telergram for one Ranger Jim Hatfield. It come in at Kent station, and I was ridin' thisaway and said I'd fetch it. Is Hatfield here?'

'Yeah, that's me,' called the Ranger.

'Throw it down on the porch,' ordered one of the guards.

The messenger quickly obeyed. Evidently he was alarmed at the show of weapons and the tough appearance of the gang which had stopped him on his way to the Dot O.

When the trio had gone, Hatfield retrieved the wire, and opened it. He read it over, and then, without comment, passed it to the curious Oden. The wire said:

THE ADJUTANT GENERAL ORDERS RANGER JIM HATFIELD TO REPORT

IMMEDIATELY AT AUSTIN TO ANSWER CHARGES OF EXTORTION LODGED BY SEVERAL MERCHANTS OF KENT, TEXAS.

'Shucks!' exclaimed Oden. 'This must be a trick of Sherrall's. I'll bet he faked this wire.'

Hatfield shrugged. 'Mebbe, but it looks like a real one. Kent's on the railroad, ain't it?'

'Yeah. It's the nearest stop to Dry River. Telergraph wires run through there, too.'

'I can detect Senator Baggett's fine hand in this,' said the Ranger. 'He got busy on the wires and lodged charges agin' me. And from what the message says, more'n one complaint come in. "Merchants of Kent," it goes. I'll have to check on this, Oden. I won't be losin' time, for we must keep a close eye on Sherrall. He's got plenty of cash from sellin' stock and lots, and he's shrewd. He'll be plannin' on how to finish us. After dark I'll sneak out and make a quick run to Paradise and Kent and see what holds. You lie doggo here till yuh hear from me. Don't put down yore guard or Pereda'll take yuh.'

The telegram from the capital frankly puzzled him. It had all the earmarks of a bona-fide wire, with stamp, numbers and destination symbols. He was sure that Madison Baggett was behind it, but the reputation of the Rangers had to be jealously upheld.

'Now, I wonder,' he mused. 'I did lose my

star at Sherrall's. S'pose somebody else used it, along with my name?'

'If they wanted yuh to get that order,' suggested Terence Oden, 'mebbe they'll let yuh out, Hatfield.'

The Ranger shook his head. 'They might. But they'd rather see me dead. Lockhart bein' free has drove Sherrall to out-and-out attack on you, Oden. I reckon Pereda sent that telegram through to throw me off. He might even hope I'd do just what I intend to—make a run out of here. If they can down me they'll do it, and them charges cover 'em enough so a lawyer like Sherrall, willin' to perjure hisself and use fake witnesses, could snake out of it.'

CHAPTER FOURTEEN

RIDE THROUGH DANGER

Dark fell over the range. Jim Hatfield checked his guns and filled the loops of spare belts with ammunition for them. He went to the near-by stable where the sorrel awaited him. Goldy was rested, and had been watered and fed. He led his horse out, saddled up, and made ready for his dangerous ride. Oden joined him, pressed his hand.

'Take care of yoreself, boy. Yuh're the best friend we got in the world, and I hate to think what'll happen to us if yuh go under. Come back soon as yuh can.'

'I'll be back,' promised Hatfield. 'We'll beat Sherrall at his own game.'

He moved off, picking up speed, and keeping a revolver cocked in one hand as he guided Goldy with the other, peering ahead for signs of his enemies. He moved on the open range, but his figure was against a fence line where thick brush grew, making it difficult to see him at any distance.

Several hundred yards out from the ranch, a horseman bore down on him, and challenged. Hatfield veered. A stab of blue-yellow flame searched for him and he fired back, swerving and picking up speed.

'There he goes!' shrieked the fellow who had glimpsed him.

'Waitin' for me,' the Ranger concluded, as he glanced back over his hunched shoulder. 'Hoped that message would drive me out so's they could take me.'

He pressed on, and the wind whistled past his bent head. Dark figures dashed in from all sides. They seemed to be everywhere, calling to one another, seeking him in the shadows. They would rush to a spot, directed by the frantic calls of one of their number, only to find that their quarry had doubled back or ridden off to the side. Hatfield's Colt blasted a path when necessary, and the swift sorrel carried him well. There were moments when he thought he was boxed, but he had the advantage over those searching for him, because he knew every horseman he met was a foe, while they were unsure, and forced to call to one another for identification.

It was a close run, and they chased him for a time, but he was out ahead. They quit the fruitless run when he lost them in the mesquite, and he swung south for the railroad.

It was so late when he came to the little settlement of Paradise that even the saloons were shut. Sherrall's office and the door of the Land and Water Company were padlocked, the interiors dark.

He paused to read a large poster nailed to a board fence around a vacant lot. The letters were large and black against the white paper background, and here and there a line was accented in red ink. By the flickering oil lamplight he could make out the import:

FREE EATS! BIG BARBECUE!
FREE BEER!!!!
DEDICATION CEREMONIES AT PARADISE DAM, THURS., AUG. 6TH. GRAND OPENING OF PARADISE WATER COMPANY's TREMENDOUS IRRIGATION PROJECT. A FEW LOTS REMAIN TO BE SOLD TO THE FORTUNATE FIRST COMERS. FREE CHANCE ON A CHOICE SITE TO EACH PURCHASER OF STOCK. SPEECHES

BY NOTED CITIZENS INCLUDING SENATOR MADISON BAGGETT AND COUNSELLOR LUTHER SHERRALL, FAMED PROMOTER OF PARADISE COMPANIES AND WELL-KNOWN PHILANTHROPIST. EXCURSION TRAINS FROM EL PASO AND FROM POINTS EAST. FARE FREE TO ALL WHO PURCHASE LAND OR STOCK!!!!!!

There were time-tables of the special trains running to Kent for the party.

'Well, doag my hide if Sherrall ain't mighty shore of hisself,' ruminated the Ranger, as he backed away into the shadows to pick up Goldy. 'Sounds like a swell blow-out. Reckon I can't afford to miss it. He'll sell a bunch of land and stock thataway. I wonder if he'll go through with it, now?'

He was inclined to believe that Sherrall would; in fact, that the Counsellor would be forced to see the affair through as highly advertised. To delay it, or call it off would seriously undermine public confidence in the venture.

The road south to Kent, at which the railroad stopped, was open, and he turned the sorrel along it.

Dawn was up when he reached the town. It was larger than Paradise, a beef-shipping center, and handled freight for the ranches within a hundred miles radius. There were large stores and hotels, eating places, and streets of homes. Down the tracks from the passenger and freight depots were corrals, some filled with cattle.

The night telegraph operator and ticket agent was leaning back in his swivel chair, his feet on the desk, green eyeshade pulled down. He started awake as Hatfield spoke to him through the wicket. He accepted the telegram which the Ranger had received at the Dot O, and studied it.

'Yes, mister, that come in here from Austin. Instructions with it said yuh might be found at the Dot O Ranch or in Dry River—Paradise, they call her now. I got another one here for yuh, too. Tried to deliver it, but the kid who run over with it said he was turned back. Some hombres took the wire from him and said they'd deliver it, but they looked ugly, he told me. Did yuh get it?'

'No. When'd the second one come?'

'Couple hours after the first. Here's a copy.'

Hatfield read the second wire, addressed to him at Dry River. It was from Captain Bill McDowell, and read:

MAN POSING AS YOU WEARING RANGER STAR ROBBING STORE-KEEPERS OF KENT YOU SAVVY WHAT TO DO WHEN YOU MEET UP WITH HIM LEAVE THE AGO TO ME LUCK

The Ranger grinned as he thought of McDowell back in Austin, making the air sulphurous with the exposition of his views.

He could see it all now. Baggett had started the complaints rolling, and Sherrall had sent an aide, wearing the stolen star on silver circle, and using Hatfield's name, to force money from Kent merchants. This trick had caused the indignant victims to hotfoot it to the station to deliver by wire their angry protests, which might provide Sherrall and his friends with a loop-hole when they had disposed of Hatfield.

As soon as McDowell had learned of the AGO's wire, he had reacted characteristically. He would protect his Rangers to the death, and he trusted Hatfield as he trusted himself.

'He's hit the nail, on the head,' mused the Ranger. 'I want my star back.'

After Sherrall had set Baggett to work to undermine Hatfield's reputation, the lawyer had been forced to attack the Dot O openly, because of Lockhart's rescue. Pereda had allowed the first wire to reach the ranch, but had stopped the reassuring message from McDowell.

The town was beginning to wake up, as the sun turned from red to golden. Shops were opening, and the smell of coffee and frying ham tinged the warming air. Taking a side street, the Ranger walked the sorrel up it. He could look through to the central plaza, a usual adjunct of most Texas towns.

Leaving Goldy at a hitch-rail, sheltered by the adobe wall of a building, he entered a restaurant and ordered ham, eggs, coffee and biscuits. He filled up with a warm, sustaining meal.

The waitress was a slim little blonde. She had a quick smile for the rugged, masculine young giant she was waiting on. Hatfield grinned back at her. He opened a conversation by complimenting her on the service and asking for a fourth cup of coffee. She lingered near the table, looking down at him in a proprietary way. There were not many customers in the place as yet, so she had time to talk.

'You a stranger in town?' she inquired.

'Yes'm. But if I'd known the place was so interestin', I'd have been here long ago.'

'Oh now, you stop!' But she was pleased and patted her light hair, held by pins in a round knot at the back of her shapely head. Her young face was bright, colored by his compliment, and the frank admiration in his eyes. 'You waddies are all the same—always trying to sweeten a girl with your silly talk. You expect to stay long?'

'I may be around a while—now I've seen you ma'am. I've herded a lot of cows the past few years. I was thinkin' of headin' for Austin and mebbe joinin' the Texas Rangers. What's yore opinion of that?'

117

'The Rangers?' A troubled look came into her blue eyes. 'Well, I've met a few, and they're all fine fellows. It's awfully dangerous work, though. Why don't you look around these parts, and settle down? A rolling stone gathers no moss, you know.'

He wanted to lead her back onto the Ranger subject.

'It's a nice town. But I sort of had my heart set on bein' a Ranger.'

'There's been a Ranger in town lately,' she told him. 'But he doesn't act like a real one. Or maybe he was drinking too much for his own good. A lot of people have been complaining.'

'Complainin'! Why, what's he been up to?'

She lowered her voice, leaning closer to his ear.

'Some people say he's forced them to pay him money for protection. Threatened them with his gun.'

'Huh! Hard to believe about a Ranger. How can they tell he's a Ranger?'

'He's got a Ranger star, and says he's one.' Hatfield's apparent doubt caused her to offer corroboration. 'Ask Mr. Haynes in the big feed store at the corner—or Mr. Mallett at the hardware shop, if you don't believe what I say.'

'Oh, I believe you, little miss.'

He patted her hand, which was conveniently close to his, and when he went out left her an extra large tip, though it was plain from the way she watched the tall, broad-shouldered figure through the door that she would have preferred his company to his money.

Haynes, the feed-store man, was reticent. He shut up tight as a clam when Hatfield broached the subject of the supposed Ranger who had taken money from him.

But Dan Mallett, the owner of the Hardware Emporium, was a different type. He was small, alert, and wore thick glasses, but behind them were keen blue eyes that missed little. His bald head gleamed in the ray of light from his front window and his lips clucked angrily when the tall stranger inquired about his trouble with the Ranger.

'Huh! I don't know who you are, young man, but I'll talk about it to every decent person who asks me! I've telegraphed a complaint to the Adjutant General, and I don't care who savvies. See this cut on my face? Well, this fool Ranger was drunk, but that's no excuse. When I refused to pay him money—he claimed it was for "protection" against some outlaws nobody ever heard of—he punched me, and a black signet ring he wore tore my cheek. Said he'd give me time to think it over, that he'd be back to collect. I told him I'd never pay such blackmail, that he could go ahead and shoot me.'

Mallett's eyes shot sparks and he had the appearance of a bantam rooster ready to defend himself.

'I always thought high of the Rangers till

119

that skunk come here,' he ended. 'If they don't bust him wide open, I'll never trust one agin.'

'What'd this polecat look like? I'm interested, because a feller that sounds just like him played the same trick on my cousin, George Haynes, down the street.'

'Oh, so yuh're Haynes' cousin! Well, this Ranger was near tall as you. He had dark hair, but his face was thinner and he needed a shave mighty bad. He wore a Ranger star and two Colts with walnut stocks and blue steel barrels. Said his handle was Jim Hatfield and he was from Austin.'

It was crude work, mused the tall officer, yet it might have sufficed had they been able to dispose of him. He thanked Mallett and went out.

There were teams entering the town, and people on foot walking beneath the wooden sun awnings. In the pens cattle bawled, and down a road on the outskirts of town moved a ragged file of cows being driven toward the corrals.

Women in sweeping skirts and deep bonnets, with market baskets on arms and children following or playing about them, emerged from their homes. Work was beginning. The stores were open, and the Texas town went busily about its affairs.

The world was a pleasant place to live in, thought the Ranger. It was natural to love life, and to shun death and trouble. People had to eat and sleep, make a living, care for their dear ones, those close to them. It was hard to rouse men to a crusade of any description.

But the Texas Rangers must be upheld in their unblemished reputation, and one man was seeking to ruin that.

'I'd like to meet up with that hombre,' Hatfield muttered.

CHAPTER FIFTEEN

INVESTIGATION

Mounted on a dusty black, a redheaded man trailed by three more riders, rode down the center of the wide street adjoining the plaza. Jim Hatfield drew back to a doorway, and recognized Red, one of Sherrall's lieutenants. The others were some of the bunch.

Red didn't see Hatfield. He turned his horse in before coming abreast of the Ranger and, dropping his reins over the rail, ducked under and went into a large honkytonk which offered liquor, the lures of the gaming table and feminine society to the weary cowboy and businessman. His men followed him. The place had its doors open though its usual denizens were still asleep, having caroused until the small hours of the morning.

Hatfield took note of the place. Its name

was the Elite. It had wide windows and batwings, and spread over a goodly area of ground, with bars and a dance annex.

A train whistled in the distance. The town of Kent seemed to prick up its ears. Urchins, drivers of wagons and buggies headed toward the station, and loafers wandered that way, shutting up their jack-knives. Red and his men also joined the procession, riding their mustangs to the tracks.

Hatfield played hide-and-seek through the town. He was watching from a vantage point across the way when the passenger train from El Paso pulled in. Several uninteresting passengers got off, but what caught the Ranger's eye was Senator Madison Baggett, escorting a knot of strangers, most of them in range clothing, but a couple wearing 'city' garb.

The Senator's pulpy face was beaming with good humor, and his fat hands waved as he offered his guests the hospitality of the city. Hatfield could hear his booming voice all the way across the street, above the hubbub of the train's arrival.

Red had come to meet Baggett. He stayed in the background but caught the Senator's eye, and as soon as possible Baggett left his group and spoke briefly with the gunny. Hatfield saw Baggett start, and wipe his forehead with an eloquent hand. The timing of Red's arrival in Kent, not long after Hatfield's own, and Baggett's reaction, made the Ranger believe that Red had brought the news concerning Lockhart's escape and the fact that Hatfield himself might be near.

After a meal, the men whom Baggett had brought with him on the train were started with a guide on the road to Paradise. Obviously they were customers of Sherrall's Land and Water Company. The Senator himself retired to the Elite, to a back suite. He turned in there, for he had been traveling for long hours.

Hatfield spent the day in Kent, keeping out of sight as far as possible, and watching for the man who was impersonating him. But it was not until late that night that his perseverance was rewarded. Baggett and Red had shown him that the Elite was the gang's headquarters in Kent, so it was chiefly the honkytonk which claimed the Ranger's attention.

The Elite warmed up with the late afternoon and evening. When dark fell it was running full blast. Students of serious drinking lined the bars. Gamesters were solemn-eyed at the tables under shaded lamps.

Cowboys and other young fellows danced with the brightly-clad, smiling dance hall girls.

Through an open window, Hatfield could see and hear Senator Baggett, at supper, in his suite. Baggett was entertaining. He had two handsomely dressed men friends at his table, and three of the prettiest of the dance hall girls as their companions. Wine was flowing freely, and the Senator was all smiles, courtly in manner with the ladies. Poetry sprang from his liquor-wet lips.

'It's great to relax for a few moments, my dear friends,' Hatfield heard him say, as he toasted his feminine partner. 'The cares of state have been heavy upon my soul these past days, and great projects claim my undivided attention.'

'Oh, Senator, I love to hear you talk!' gushed a girl.

Baggett was beaming on her when a waiter knocked and brought him a note. He read it, excused himself, and went out. Hatfield was hidden back in the shadows as the Senator emerged from a rear door of the Elite, followed by a tall fellow who had evidently sent in the note. They paused in the alley, speaking in low tones.

'I had Red send you here Carney,' the Senator said, 'because I've just learned that several things have gone sour. For one, this Hatfield you've impersonated is loose. He escaped us and he may be on his way here. For another, Lockhart was snatched from the camp at the dam, either by Oden or the Ranger—it doesn't matter which to us. You still have the Ranger badge?'

'Sure, Senator, right here.' Carney patted his pocket.

'Pin it on, then, and raise as much merry

124

Hades in the name of the Rangers as you can tonight. You did very well before, Bull. There were a dozen complaints sent to Austin. You can beat up a couple of people, but be sure they understand you're a Ranger. When you've finished, say around midnight, pull out of here and report to Sherrall in Paradise. We're collecting as many men as we can to clean up Oden and his bunch. Those are orders from the Counsellor, straight.'

'All right, Baggett,' said Carney. 'If I don't see yuh in Paradise, I'll see yuh in the other place.'

'Good boy. Luck to you. Make it real, now.'

Baggett went back to his party, and Carney slipped off down the alleyway. The trailing Ranger saw him pause under a street lamp and pin on a silver star on silver circle, emblem of the Rangers. And Carney was wearing Hatfield's revolvers.

'Bull' Carney swaggered toward the main thoroughfare, the Ranger badge glinting in the light of the street lamps. Music, the yells of merrymakers, came from the saloons. Most of the stores had closed for the night, but eating houses and drinking oases were doing a rushing business.

Around at the front of the big Elite, Carney pushed through the batwings and roughly elbowed his way to a bar.

'Red-eye!' he roared, banging the bar with the butt of one of Hatfield's pistols. 'The best red-eye in the place for a Texas Ranger! Pronto! I got work to do.'

Men stopped jostling. They drew away, giving him room. Many eyes turned toward the self-proclaimed officer. Carney downed several whiskies without pausing except to smack his lips between each. He wiped his mouth on his shirt sleeve, saluted the bartender, and went out without paying the score.

Hatfield was watching from the shadows. Carney strode down the center of the walk, knocking people out of his path. Some started to object, but seeing the Ranger star, thought better of it and hurried on their way. The tall imposter crossed the corner of the plaza, and went up on the porch of a small, square home. He rapped loudly on the door. There was a light burning in the front room, and the man who opened the door was Dan Mallett, owner of the Hardware Emporium on Main Street.

'What do yuh want?' Mallett demanded. 'Yuh better get out of here. Yuh've made enough trouble!'

Bravely the little merchant stood up to the armed Carney, who weighed twice as much as he. Carney hit him, slapped him in the mouth. Mallett's spectacles fell off. His lip burst, and blood smeared his chin. He was thrown off balance by the force of the blow, and as he stooped to pick up his glasses, Carney kicked him and Mallett fell over on his side.

'Yuh little skunk!' snarled Bull Carney, jumping on him with both feet. 'Yuh been lyin' about me—me, Jim Hatfield, the best Ranger in Texas. Yuh wouldn't give me any money, but now yu'll pay or I'll pull every inch of hide off'n yore carcass!'

Mallett sought to rise. His lips were set and though he was in agony from the kicks and punches dealt him, he gasped:

'Go on, kill me, cuss yuh! I won't pay no blackmail. Yuh're a disgrace to the State!'

Hatfield was almost upon Carney now. He was on the porch, and Carney, intent upon beating Mallett, did not hear the faint creak as the big man approached, his gray-green eyes dark with the icy gleam of an Arctic sea.

It had gone beyond the local trouble which had brought Jim Hatfield to Dry River. While he still meant to save Oden and the scattered ranchers who had been bilked of their water company by Luther Sherrall, he had a greater mission now. Sherrall had set Bull Carney to work and the Rangers must be vindicated, for they enjoyed a peculiar reputation in Texas.

Protectors of the decent citizens, though few in numbers, the Rangers brought the Law to the vast reaches of the mighty Lone Star State. It was almost a sacred obligation to protect that reputation. It transcended any practical case of robbery or killing.

Dan Mallett saw Hatfield glide through the doorway. His widening eyes, racked with pain as Carney kicked him with sharp-toed boots, raking back across his ribs with his big Mexican spurs, lighted as he recognized the silent, mighty rescuer.

Bull Carney, breathing hard, his tobacco-stained teeth bared in a snarl, noted Mallett's look. He swung with a curse, checked at his brutal work.

Carney had not met Hatfield. Bull was one of the gang whom Sherrall had recently imported, and was not known in Kent or Dry River. He did not realize that the rugged fellow watching him with cold eyes was the Ranger he was impersonating, but Hatfield impressed him.

'What yuh want, mister?' he snapped. 'Yuh're interferin' with the Law. See this?' He tapped a finger to the silver star, pinned to his sweated shirt. 'I'm a Texas Ranger and I'm givin' this hombre what he's got comin'. So go on about yore business or I'll take you next.'

'Take me now, Carney,' drawled Hatfield. 'Those are my guns yuh been bangin' on the bar, and that's my badge, yuh've dirtied up by touchin' it.'

Carney blinked.

His mouth opened as he took a deep breath, then he swallowed. But he pulled himself together.

'Yuh're a liar!' he said. 'My handle's Jim Hatfield. I'm goin' to run yuh in and lock yuh up.'

Hatfield, booted feet set wide, slouched just inside Mallett's doorway. The little storekeeper had come up on one knee, was supporting himself with a hand to the floor. Blood welled from his cut lip, and his clothing had been torn by Carney's spur points. But there was an eager gleam in Mallett's intent eyes.

'Yuh made a big error when yuh flouted the Rangers, Carney,' went on Hatfield. 'It was a fatal mistake to let Baggett and Sherrall talk yuh into it. Nobody but a fool would have dared it.'

The Colts still remained in the Ranger's holsters. His long hands hung easily at his sides, and he was relaxed. But he was watching Bull Carney's eyes. A harshness flicked into them and Carney whipped up a revolver, the explosion banging through Mallett's front room.

CHAPTER SIXTEEN

POLITICO

Jim Hatfield's hand was a blur as he drew and fired. He had expected Bull Carney to panic, and had watched his eyes for the move to be telegraphed, so had been ready for it.

The explosions of the big revolvers seemed

joined in one, yet the first had come ahead of the second shot.

Splinters licked up as a .45 caliber slug drove into Mallett's flooring, between spread feet. That one had been aimed too low, and the gun had gone off because the man behind it had been shocked by the violent, tearing lead from his opponent's weapon.

It was a strange sensation for Hatfield, to be shooting against his own finely kept, perfectly balanced Colts. But he was such a master of firearms that he was able to give Carney the advantage of the draw and the use of the best of weapons.

Bull Carney's gun arm dropped, his mouth opened like that of a dying fish. The shock of the lead in his chest had thrown him back as though a giant had hit him with a hammer. For a breath his reflexes held him up. But the directives of his brain had ceased, and his muscles went lax, all over, in death. He became a limp mass of flesh, and piled up on the mat, dead before he hit.

'Beautiful—beautiful shot!' cried Dan Mallett. He came up on his feet, jumping up and down in the excitement. 'I never seen anything like it. Yuh must be—'

He broke off, and waited as Hatfield took back his blue steel, walnut-stocked Colts, and checked them over to make sure they were unharmed. He reloaded the one with which Carney had tried to kill him. He removed the

Ranger emblem from Carney's shirt, and pinned it on his own.

'Yes, I knew it!' cried Mallett, rushing to pump his arm and congratulate him. 'Yuh're a Ranger—a real one!'

Hatfield nodded. 'This hombre went around sayin' he was one, but he wasn't, Mallett. Him and some other pole-cats used my badge and guns to give the Rangers a black eye. But I'd as soon yuh kept this to yoreself, for the time bein'.'

'Whatever yuh say, Ranger. But folks ought to savvy this garbage ain't a real officer. He's done you boys a lot of harm here.'

'We'll fix that.'

Hatfield turned, to see if the shots had disturbed Kent. But music from the saloons, the fact that often enough drunken men fired their guns into the air in exuberation, had caused the sounds to go unnoticed.

'Yuh're all right, Mallett,' Hatfield told the merchant. 'Yuh got a man's nerve. I heard yuh stand up to Carney. Now I'm here on important business, but when it's cleared up, yuh can give the Rangers a hand by spreadin' yore story. I'm Hatfield, the officer Carney posed as bein'.'

He had work to do. Mallett was eager to help, willing to do whatever Hatfield asked. He had a hand cart in his stable, and placed Carney's body in it.

Hatfield told him what to do after that, and

Mallet nodded with enthusiasm.

The Ranger slipped away in the darkness. He went around to the rear of the Elite, which was steaming away at full tilt.

The Senator and his party were still at it, the empty champagne bottles standing like a squad of soldiers on the white tablecloth, the silver service shining in the lamplight. Senator Baggett was enjoying himself hugely.

Guarding the door into the hall were two gentlemen in neat black clothing. Their coats bulged at their right hips, where their guns hung ready for use. They were two of Sherrall's town gunmen, hard-eyed, but quiet and efficient. Hatfield had seen them before, in Paradise.

He waited just outside the door which led into the rear street. After a time a couple of customers appeared from the front bar, staggering slightly. The eyes of the strong-arm men turned toward them, and Hatfield stepped into the corridor.

A piano and several violins were at it in the dance annex. The floors shook with the stamp of heavy feet engaged in what was supposed to be the light fantastic. Girls and men were shouting, and a voice was shrieking in a whisky tenor:

I'm on-ly a bird-d in a gil-ded ca-hage . . .

Hatfield was six feet away when the nearer

sentry swung back, and sighted him. He recognized the Ranger, and his whole quiet being was suddenly galvanized.

'Hey—hey, Dinny!' he squeaked, thrown off by the apparition before him. Even as he spoke he threw back the flap of his coat with a swift hand.

It froze at his hip. Then both paws started slowly reaching for the ceiling. He stared into the muzzle of the Ranger Colt, and Dinny, swinging at his partner's exclamation, made no attempt to draw as a second pistol menaced him. Both men stood rigid, fear in their eyes.

'See that broom closet, boys?' said Hatfield. 'Step up there and get inside. Long as yuh stay in there quiet yuh got a chance to keep on breathin' for a while.'

He dropped the latch on them and pushed an iron bolt into position. Then he hurried to the door of the private room in which Baggett was having his party, opened it, and stepped inside.

The girl with the Senator saw the tall, quiet man. She laughed, and nodded toward Hatfield, and Baggett, with a frown, removed his arm from about her wasp waist and swung around with a sharp reprimand.

'You ought to knock before coming into a gentleman's—'

He nearly fell off his chair. His whole face went lax, and his eyes flickered.

'You!'

133

'Good evenin', Senator,' said Hatfield softly. 'Sorry to disturb yuh, but it's important. Affairs of state. Quis custodiet ipsos custodes?—"who'll guard the guards?" I think that's how it goes. I spent two years at college myself. S'pose we step outside so's we won't bother the ladies.'

Baggett pulled himself together. He cleared his throat.

'I'm very busy at the moment, sir,' he said. 'Why not in the morning?'

'Oh, he's a Texas Ranger!' exclaimed a girl. 'See his badge!'

'Time's fleetin', Senator,' reminded Hatfield. 'I give yuh my word I'll let yuh come back to yore guests in a few minutes.'

Baggett rose, his ayes riveted on Hatfield. He was in deathly fear, but he had seen the Ranger in action. The big officer's quickness, his escape, the damage he had done to Sherrall and the Senator, single-handed, and Baggett's natural cowardice all made it impossible for him to resist.

Hatfield held the door for him, with respectful politeness. The Senator stepped into the hall, and his wildly roving eyes hunted for his guards, but they were locked in the closet.

'This way, Senator,' drawled the Ranger.

He steered the quivering politico out the rear door, and walked him up the alley.

These were important moments for

Hatfield, for Texas. The saving of Oden and his ranchers was but one angle. There was the matter of hundreds of other people, decent citizens of the state, like Jervis and Tate, and those exploited workers at the dam who had built it with sweat and toil.

'I warn you, Hatfield,' blustered Baggett, looking gingerly back over his shoulder as he waddled ahead of the tall officer, 'I'll make trouble for you. I have influence in Austin. I'll have you broken, fired! I know your commander, Captain McDowell.'

'Yeah, and he savvies you, too, Senator. That makes it fine. I ain't goin' to hurt yuh unless yuh make a move agin me. Don't try to pull that popgun yuh got in yore pocket.'

'I—I won't. I won't stoop to the indignity of force.' Baggett was quivering. His teeth rattled so that it was hard to speak clearly. 'Where are you t-t-taking me?' he demanded.

'Turn to the right up the next side way.'

They moved to the main street, crossing to the plaza, and thence to a large watering trough. Baggett stopped, to stare at a dead man propped in a hand cart. Affixed to the front of the cart by tacks was a large white cardboard placard, with bold letters printed on it in black ink:

THIS IS *NOT* A TEXAS RANGER.

Dan Mallett had made that for Hatfield. It

had taken him but a few minutes at his home, where he had a stack of used window cards, and he had printed it on the back of a display sign.

'Carney!' stammered Baggett.

'He drew and fired, so I had to kill him,' explained Hatfield in a gentle voice. 'The Rangers always give a man a chance, Senator, before they shoot, no matter who he is. I'd even give Sherrall and you such a break.'

'What do you mean?'

The liquor had left Baggett's brain, driven away by the awful fright which possessed him. He could see the sheen of Hatfield's eyes upon him, the shape of the mighty man who dominated him.

'Yuh've cheated Oden and his friends,' Hatfield accused inexorably. 'Yuh've worked them pore fellers at the dam and won't give 'em their hard-earned money. I like Jervis and Tate, and the other folks yuh mean to rob, with yore Water Company. Once yuh got 'em here, yuh'll charge 'em till they're broke. Then yuh'll sell to new victims. It's all nice and legal, of course, Sherrall bein' a lawyer. Only in gettin' control, Sherrall killed a man, and yuh're abettin' him. I give yuh my word as a Ranger that I'll never be downed till you and yore pards have paid.'

'What do you expect me to do?' Baggett asked sullenly.

The Ranger's long-fingered hand vised on

the fat wrist. He could feel the heavy pounding of Baggett's pulse, the trembling of his creeping flesh.

'I'll tell yuh,' he said flatly. 'But if yuh cross me, Baggett, I'll foller yuh to the hot place and back and make yuh answer for it. I'll have my eye on yuh.'

'And what have I to gain if I do as you say?'

'Yore hide, for one thing—and my guarantee as a Ranger that yuh'll get off easy for helpin' the Law. Judges take that into account at trials. You ain't so bad off. Yuh haven't killed anybody that I know of, and yore main crime is workin' with Sherrall. I got to save these folks that he's cheatin', above all.'

At last Baggett nodded. 'All right. I'm helpless, Hatfield. I'll do what you want.'

Hatfield gave detailed instructions. When Baggett heard what he had to do, he shivered and balked, but the steel grip convinced him.

'But—what about tonight?' he asked querulously. 'Sherrall will hear yuh snatched me out of the Elite, then released me. He may get suspicious.' Baggett studied the rugged face, seemed to be weighing the dangers— Hatfield, Sherrall. 'He'll have me killed if he gets a hint of what's up. I'll be in danger, too, when I speak. Sherrall may shoot me when I'm on the platform.'

'I'll take care of Sherrall and the rest,' the Ranger promised. 'As for tonight, tell him I visited yuh and questioned yuh, but yuh lied

137

and threw me off the track. Warn him I'm dangerous, that he's got to see I'm finished. Sherrall will believe that. He needs you as part of his front, and he won't think yuh'd put yoreself in the hands of the law.'

Baggett shook his head, still fearful.

'To cinch it,' said Hatfield, 'wait a few minutes, then give the alarm. Say I'm around, that yore boys are to gun me and capture or kill me.'

'Good.' Baggett nodded. 'That may do the trick.'

Hatfield released the Senator, and picked up the sorrel. He paused to thank Dan Mallett, then rode toward the Elite. Red and several of his gunnies emerged from the big honkytonk, and Hatfield showed himself under a street lamp.

'There he is!'

That was Madison Baggett shrieking, pointing the Ranger's way.

Red ran to the sidewalk, ducking under the rail, followed by his men. They opened fire at once but the Ranger was moving fast, and streaked through the shadows. He cut around the west side of the town, hit the open road, and made for Paradise, the hue and cry behind him.

CHAPTER SEVENTEEN

MENACE

Early dawn was approaching when Hatfield reached the outskirts of Paradise. A gray streak showed in the sky on his right.

He made camp in some woods on a height overlooking the settlement on the river, where he spread his poncho after seeing to Goldy. He catnapped until nearly noon. By then the heat had grown so intense that it awakened him and he lay there, watching the apparently deserted little town below.

He swept the scene with his field-glasses, but saw no activity. It was too hot for men to stir about much in the middle of the day. The door of the offices of the Paradise Land & Water Co. was standing open, but no signs of life showed there nor in Luther Sherrall's near-by law office.

Goldy was well back, hidden from the dirt road which climbed the slope from the valley stream which meandered westward toward the far-off mountains. The main route to the outer world ran south, through Kent, where the railroad drew the traffic.

The clop-clop of a couple of mustangs, coming from the west on the rutted trail, turned Hatfield's attention that way. He lay flat, chin resting on his left forearm. His right was close to his Colt.

He could just glimpse a little stretch of the trail through a leafy vista. Two men he did not know appeared. They pulled up, at the crest of the hill.

'There's the shebang below, Benny,' the Ranger heard one of them say. 'Whew, ain't it hot!'

'Shore is,' agreed Benny, puffing. 'And we've come far enough, Ted. Pereda sent word to wait till it got dark before we reported at the Company's office. We can lie in the bush till night. I could do with some shut-eye.'

'Me, too.'

They dismounted. Hatfield could no longer see them, but he heard the cracklings of the dry brush and grass as they pushed in to find a shady spot in which to sleep. They settled down, and after a while the Ranger heard snoring. Their mustangs kept stamping restlessly, now and then snuffling or whinnying a plaint against the heat.

Two hours later, several Mexican vaqueros came along the trail. The point at which Benny and Ted had entered the chaparral attracted them, and they stopped. Then some of them got down and, with weapons ready, moved as silently as possible toward the bivouac of the first two men.

'Reach, senores!'

There were curses. Then a delighted

voice—Benny's—exclaimed:

'Why, if it ain't Chihuahua Pete! Yuh old sidewinder, what you doin' in these parts? Same thing as us, I'll bet.'

'Senor Benn-y!'

It was a reunion of old trailmates, evidently. The silent, listening Ranger could hear them as bottles were brought out and the two parties merged.

'Yeah, Pereda sent for us, too, Chihuahua,' Benny was saying after a while. 'I ain't worked with him since we all pulled that bank job outside El Paso last summer. He's a good hombre.'

'Si, si. What he weesh, you savvy?'

'Oh, it's strong-arm work, I understand. Got a bunch of cowmen he wants to put the fear of the devil into.'

Throughout the afternoon, more riders arrived, until Hatfield counted fifteen, including those he had first seen. They were armed bravos, many of them Mexicans, and all were waiting for night before descending on the town.

'Sherrall's pullin' in reinforcements,' the Ranger mused. 'If fifteen showed on this goat track, there'll be a bunch more on the other route.'

It was serious. Through his outlaw lieutenants, Sherrall had sent out a call for assistance. He could hire many guns for a few days at comparatively small cost, temporary help.

'I reckon Baggett knew of this,' Hatfield decided. 'He's butterin' his bread on both sides, just in case. If Sherrall downs me, Baggett'll be safe, and if I down Sherrall, he's got a loop-hole so's he'll get off easy.'

That did not suprise him. The Senator always thought of Number One first. Probably he had been aware of Sherrall's plan to bring in overwhelming strength so that nothing would go wrong during the ceremonies at the dam.

At last the ruby red sun dropped behind the western mountains. The heat still held, and the world was lifeless, without a breeze to stir the dry seed pods of the chaparral. In the stillness, sounds carried far, and clearly, and the Ranger had to wait until the men ahead of him moved down the rocky trail to cross the stream into Paradise.

There were many people around town, some Sherrall's regulars, the others strangers. Hatfield left Goldy hidden out from the settlement and approached on foot. Men were collecting at the Land and Water Company offices. Most of them were outside, smoking and talking on the sidewalk.

'Looks like it's goin' to be interestin',' decided the Ranger. 'If I can get close enough, I'd like to attend that meetin'.'

He knew the layout of the place. The building in which the company had its quarters was one-storied, with a low, flat roof. But there were watchers in Tin Can Alley, and it would be out of the question to approach from the front.

'Up above's the only way,' he thought, noting that next to this goal stood a slightly higher edifice.

He stayed back of the ragged line of sheds, barns and stables behind the structures on the main thoroughfare until he found what he was looking for—a short, thick length of plank which he borrowed from a pile lying at the rear of a barn. Leaning at the shadowed corner of a shed on the side away from the Golden Gates saloon, Hatfield watched his chance.

When the two sentries at the rear of the offices were looking the other way, he flitted across the alley, to a dark side way between two stores. By means of a drainpipe he reached the roof of the taller building he had selected, and drew his plank up after him. Keeping low, he crept to the other side and, hidden except from directly below, set the plank and went over to the next roof. By judicious timing he finally crossed onto the Land and Water Company's roof, and pulled in his portable bridge.

He did not have long to wait, as he lay flat on the warm roof. Luther Sherrall came from the Golden Gates where he had just dined. Enrique Pereda, white teeth showing in a grin, swaggered at the Counsellor's side. The gangling Red was there, too, and other important aides of Sherrall, called in for this meeting.

'Gentlemen, good evening!' Sherrall greeted the men awaiting him. Armed bodyguards protected him as he tapped his heavy cane on the wooden sidewalk. 'Come inside,' he invited.

On the roof, Hatfield lay just over the open window where Sherrall's desk stood, and he could hear the voices below. There were heavy shufflings and a rumble of talk as the men settled themselves in the office—coarse jests and oaths flung between friends of the open road.

'All right men, let's have your attention,' ordered Sherrall. He sneezed several times, having taken some snuff, and as his visitors quieted down, he then began to speak to them.

'There's a difficult situation here, boys. A gang of crazy cowmen have been making trouble for our company. They're led by a galoot named Terence Oden, owner of the Dot O Ranch. He has some friends with him but the opposition is not too strong. I've been patient with this Oden but he's made a nuisance of himself, and he's out of bounds. Oden and his whole crew must be cleaned out like a nest of rats.

'Not all of you know the ropes here, or the country, but Enrique Pereda and others who are familiar with all the ins and outs of the business will lead you. Day after tomorrow I'm throwing a big party at the dedication ceremonies of a dam I've built northwest of here. There'll be several hundreds of people present, many of them customers to whom I want to sell land and water stock. I must see this whole thing through.

'On the other hand, I know Oden may try to start a fuss, but everything must be quiet and look right, for we don't want to frighten prospective buyers. Until the party's over, you'll simply hold Oden and his men off. Then we'll go after him hammer and tongs and show him who's boss.'

'What's the pay?' asked one of the new men.

'Three dollars a day and keep, while you work.'

'I heard there was a Texas Ranger workin' these parts, Counsellor,' someone else drawled.

'There is,' answered Sherrall. 'I'll pay anyone a thousand dollars for his scalp, but his hash is settled just the same. This show is legal. You know I'm a lawyer, and everything is on my side. I'll pay a five-hundred-dollar bonus for Oden, and the same goes for one Bud Lockhart, who at present is hiding out at the Dot O.'

Pereda was introduced.

'Bueno, vaqueros,' he greeted them. 'We work togezzer. You weel fin' me eas-y eef you fight well, but I am Satan on wheel' eef not. And I am een ze van when zere's a scrap. No one say Pereda ees cow-ard. Some of my boys weel lead you to our camp at ze dam, where you stay teel I send ordaires.'

'I want you to slip out of town quietly,' broke in Sherrall. 'No drinking and ruckus-raising until this job is finished.'

When the rank and file had been dismissed, sliding away from Paradise under command of experienced Company men, Pereda, Red, and two or three other chiefs conferred with Luther Sherrall.

'We've got to keep Oden off, boys, till the party's over,' the Counsellor repeated. 'And that Ranger may try to make a nuisance of himself. He's at Kent now, I think. Red says he managed to down Bull Carney, and I have word from Baggett that he tried to threaten him, but Baggett doesn't believe he can get far. We've discredited him at Austin and he'll never get back there to report.

'We can use the Dot O handily, and any other spread that may fall into our hands. They're worth real money with the dam completed, and some will sell for a song when the going gets tough. With Oden and the present owners dead, I expect to be able to buy them, for there are ways to force the heirs. When the fall rains fill the reservoir, this range'll be mighty valuable.'

'Why don't we go after Oden right now, and

put him out of action before the party?' growled Red.

'For good reasons, Red my boy. It would raise a big fuss, some would escape, the news would spread and bring in more lawmen, and alarm our customers. No, it's much better to keep things as they are till we've hooked our clients. I can't call off the celebration, since it's been too highly advertised, and many are already in Kent and on their way here.'

'What about zees Lock-hart, Senor Counsellor?' asked Pereda.

Sherrall did not at once reply. He sneezed.

'He must be dealt with, Enrique,' he finally said firmly.

'We hol' ze workaires, too?' asked Pereda. 'Zey mak' fuss.'

'Certainly. You'll herd them off in the hills till the party's finished. A few armed guards can keep them down.'

'Zey want zeir pay.'

'They'll be glad to get away with their hides, Enrique. Each one will sign a receipt in full before he's allowed to leave.'

'Bueno. I put zem in leetle gulch a mile west of camp. Red and half a doz-en weel hold zem.'

Sherrall gave a few more instructions. Then the confab broke up, the Counsellor going back to the Golden Gates, Pereda riding off in the direction of the Dot O, and Red taking command of the forces in Paradise.

Hatfield waited until the place quieted down before making a careful way to the street. Then he returned to where he had left Goldy. He was planning on how to counter the enemy's moves, to save the ranchers of Dry River, the exploited workers, and the prospective new victims of Sherrall's land and water combine.

Hatfield wished to break through to the Dot O before the dawn came, and he headed the golden sorrel for Oden's.

CHAPTER EIGHTEEN

INTO POSITION

Pereda's line was farther out than it had been when Jim Hatfield had ridden the gauntlet before. A sentinel challenged him in the darkness, then opened fire, but the Ranger was galloping full-tilt toward the speck of light which marked the Dot O ranchhouse.

The swift sorrel carried him, zigzagging, safely through to the yard, and he dismounted. Oden rushed to him to grip his hand.

'Hatfield! Mighty glad yuh come! I was gettin' worried about yuh.'

'I'm all right,' assured the Ranger, 'and I've learned a lot, Oden, since I left. But I'd like a drink and a bite to eat mighty well.'

'The place is yores, Ranger.'

Oden took him to the kitchen, and they sat down while the officer ate and drank.

'How's Lockhart?' asked Hatfield.

'He's almost well. Good food and plenty of sleep have done wonders for the boy. Him and Lily—' Oden scratched his head.

Hatfield nodded. 'He's a fine young feller. If yuh ask me, Oden, they're both lucky. Couldn't either one do better.'

'That's right. He's no cowman, but he's smart and a decent hombre if ever I met one. Pereda's gang ain't charged us at all since yuh left. Baxter's here, with his boys, and three more of my friends—O'Connor of the Turkey Track, Willings of the Square Four, and King Lyden of the One-Two.

'They all brought fightin' men with 'em and broke through. Baxter and some of the others wanted to go out after Pereda and fight it to a finish, but I didn't figger we ought to go off half-cocked. Yuh told me to stick here and I done it.'

'That's fine, Oden. Lot of good men would have been killed or hurt bad if yuh'd charged 'em. They'd have had the advantage if yuh rode into the open. I've got things worked out and I need yore aid, with all yuh can scrape up in the way of scrappers.'

As the Ranger consumed his meal, he gave Oden a quick picture of all that had occurred, and began detailing for the ranch chieftain his instructions for the coming great battle against Sherrall and his forces.

Oden's keen eyes lighted and he smacked a fist into his hand with a curse of joy.

'Ranger, yuh're a wonder! When do we start?'

'Party's day after tomorrer. I'll take Lockhart and three picked young waddies who can stand a hard run and a fight at the end. You'll have command of yore neighbors. I want yuh to smash out, and feint, keep feintin' and drawin' Pereda and his gang till Pereda gets the call and turns, as I've fixed it he will. Then yuh can drive through to the dam.'

Oden repeated his orders, memorizing them so as not to forget anything.

Dawn was near, so the Ranger went to bed, safe behind alert guards about the big ranch.

Hatfield slept for several hours, gaining strength for the coming struggle against Sherrall. It was near noon when he rose, washed up, and strolled to the kitchen. Lily Oden smiled at him, and Bud Lockhart, helping her with her work, ran to seize the Ranger's hand, greeting him with the deepest joy.

'I heard you'd made it, Jim! I'm mighty happy to see you. I feel fine now. You saved my life, and I'll never be able to make it up to you.'

'Yuh can do it by helpin' me pin Sherrall to the wall,' the Ranger assured. 'Yuh're the one man who'll finish him, Bud.'

'Sit down,' ordered Lily. 'I have some pancake batter ready, and hot coffee.'

The Ranger consumed two dozen pancakes with sugar syrup and home-made butter, and several cups of steaming coffee. Then he rolled a quirly, and went up front.

Oden's rancher neighbors were about, sturdy Texas ranchers of Dry River. They all shook hands with the big Ranger, whose star glinted in the sunlight from the windows.

'They're worth savin',' mused Hatfield.

These men had pioneered this country. Their Dry River Association had thought up the idea of the dam and had tried to put it through, but Luther Sherrall had taken it from them, had stolen the fruits of their labors.

All were well aware that had it not been for the Ranger they would have been destroyed, one by one, along with Lockhart, and Sherrall would have triumphed.

During the afternoon, Hatfield made his preparations. From among the waddies he picked three who seemed to fill his bill, rangy young fellows with a reckless look in their eyes, and self-confident, yet whose answers to his apparently aimless questions showed intelligence and a willingness to follow him as a leader.

An expert judge of men, Hatfield knew what he wanted, and found the right men after a careful hunt. He sent them to sleep until he was ready for them. Lockhart, too, rested in the afternoon.

Oden had plenty of weapons and ammunition—and to spare. For everybody had brought at least two guns, and many had carried in extra shotguns and carbines, with belts of bullets for them.

The Ranger collected what he needed. When dark fell, he roused Lockhart and his trio of cowboys and told them to eat. Mustangs were carefully chosen. The guns were distributed evenly so that no one animal would have to carry too much extra weight, and around ten P.M. the Ranger and his crew said good-by to Oden and others watching them start off.

Lily stood in the shadows. Bud Lockhart kissed her.

'Be careful of yourself, Bud!' Hatfield heard her say. 'Come back safe and sound.'

The Ranger took the lead. He disposed his men with several yards between horses, keeping Lockhart in the center, a few feet behind him. He didn't want any harm to come to the engineer, his star witness against Sherrall, and Lockhart was not the horseman and expert with guns that the others were.

Pereda's ring challenged them, well away from the Dot O. There was a brief skirmish in the night, as wild slugs whistled through the air, and then they were through. The Ranger galloped along, leading his men around to the north of the ranch, then turning west and south for the dam.

Lockhart and the cowboys knew the country. The engineer had surveyed through it, while the waddies had chased cows in the foot-hills and gullies. They set their course for the upper river, and before dawn had crossed it and were working slowly down a ridge, screened by fringes of brush and scrub pines.

The engineer thought he knew exactly where the gulch mentioned by Pereda lay, and led them close to it. As gray fingers streaked the eastern sky, the Ranger left his boys in a patch of woods and crept forward to reconnoiter.

On hands and knees, he crawled to the edge of a small cut. He could scent tobacco smoke on the breeze and, peeking through openings in the chaparral, he saw the glow of a small camp-fire. A man was beside it, waiting for the coffee he was making to boil. His saddle and warbag were near-by, and his shotgun was within easy reach.

The man was Red, Sherrall's strong-arm lieutenant in charge. He was at the opening to the little gulch, and under the jut of a clay bank guards from the dam were sleeping. The captive workmen were somewhere further back in the hills.

Evidently Red did not expect any trouble, for he was alone on guard duty. The horses were picketed fifty yards away, among the trees. The Ranger stole back, collected his fighters, and gave them final orders.

They moved in on foot. Hatfield went around to the gap, the point of danger. Daylight was rapidly coming on. He could see Red more plainly now, squatted beside the little camp-fire.

Hatfield gave the men with him time to get into position. A stone rolled down the opposite bank, and Red quickly glanced around, a hand reaching toward his gun. Hatfield had told a Dot O waddy to draw the sentry's attention, and the stone had done the trick.

With the streak of a charging panther, the Ranger rushed the last few yards, and as the startled Red cursed and started to get to his feet, Hatfield was on him, covering him with a gun, his cowboy shirt as red as blood in the camp-fire light.

'Cuss it!' gasped Red.

His hands went up, but he was quick of thought. Before the Ranger could warn him to keep silent he yelled at the top of his voice. His cries roused the sleeping renegades. But by then, the three cowboys and Lockhart were sliding down into the camp, guns up.

'Reach!'

The men that Red had with him as guards were recruits, gunnies just imported by Sherrall and Pereda. They had anticipated no trouble from the cowed, unarmed workers, hidden in the hills.

One sought to get his Colt into action. A cowboy fired, the blue-yellow flash stabbing straight at the enemy. The gunman fell back, clutching his shoulder, shrieking in pain. The others threw up their hands—and the brief conflict was over.

'Tie 'em up, boys, and keep 'em quiet,' ordered Hatfield.

There was little chance that against the wind the single explosion would carry to the camp at the dam, over a mile off. But to be sure, the Ranger sent a cowboy to watch the trail in that direction.

The workmen whose labor had constructed the river dam were startled, awakened by the fight. The dawn had come, rosy over the wilderness, so they recognized Bud Lockhart, whom they knew and trusted. He had been a prisoner with them.

'Where's Murphy?' asked Bud, when he had quickly explained that the Texas Ranger had set them free.

'Pereda shot him dead, Bud,' growled Shane, a foreman who had taken Murphy's place as leader of the crew. 'Murphy led the revolt. He managed to snatch a gun from a guard and we fought 'em, but they killed Murph and wounded two more of the boys. If we ever get our hands on 'em—' Shane's black eyes snapped, and his bearded face worked with his fury.

'I got guns for yuh, Shane,' said the Ranger coolly. 'However, in case I hand 'em out to yuh I want yore promise yuh'll obey my orders. There ain't to be any shootin' unless I give the word.'

Shane frowned at him. 'A Ranger, huh? Say, we're mighty glad yuh come, but we ain't had such a good deal from the Law. We been left to rot here.'

'This is Jim Hatfield, Shane,' spoke up Lockhart. 'He snatched me from Pereda and saved my life. He'll see that everyone is treated fairly.'

They were impressed by the tall, rugged officer. Shane nodded.

'Reckon yuh're right, Bud. We're shore of you, and if you say he's It, that goes.'

'Lockhart'll be in command of you gents,' drawled Hatfield. 'What he tells yuh to do is what I want yuh to do, savvy? Don't go hogwild and spoil the game. Obey his orders. I'm goin' to be mighty busy below and I don't want any slips.'

Arms and ammunition, from stores brought in and guns taken from the prisoners, were distributed to the angry workers, who had been driven and cheated by Sherrall and his gang. Hatfield left them in Lockhart's charge, and rode toward the camp.

The sun was up when he paused on a crest, unshipping his field-glasses to check the enemy's position. The shacks stood as before, save that flags and bunting decorated them, and where the shade would fall in the afternoon, on the west side of the stream, a wooden platform had been erected. It also was draped with pennants and red-white-and-blues.

Barbecue pits had been dug and cooks were busy dressing whole sides of beef, making ready for the expected crowd. There was a booth where lots and water stock were to be sold. A few of Pereda's camp guards were about, their weapons discreetly out of sight beneath their shirts.

Cheyenne Driscoll, hors de combat, crippled by Ranger lead, lay in his tent. But Pereda was away, no doubt with his fighting line between the camp and the Dot O. Some flat wagons and other vehicles in which equipment and food had been brought were in a park below. One large truck was still loaded with kegs of beer.

'Everything's got to be timed just so,' the Ranger mused, 'or all perdition'll bust loose here.'

He was depending on Terence Oden, on Bud Lockhart and the workers, as well as on Baggett.

'The Senator will be fine so long as he figgers I'll win,' he thought. 'I'll have to jolt him a bit before he starts speakin'.'

CHAPTER NINETEEN

SQUEEZE

For part of the time Hatfield had to wait, he busied himself drawing a facsimile of a Texas Ranger's star on a piece of paper. Finished, he folded it, and slipped it in his shirt pocket.

Sherrall's cooks were spitting the big slabs of beef, hanging them over the wood-fire pits. Long tables made of planks and sawhorses stood ready for the guests, and the beer kegs were being arranged in the shade so that drinks might be dispensed. Around ten o'clock the first wagonloads of guests began pulling in from Paradise. Every sort of wheeled vehicle had been pressed into service—flat wagons with boards from side to side for seats and flimsy canvas to shade off the sun, buggies, surreys, gigs. Some men arrived on horseback. There were some women in the various parties, ladies in wide sweeping hoopskirts and bonnets, who carried dainty colored parasols.

Hatfield waited as the crowd collected, spreading over the camp grounds. The wind brought him the scent of roasting juicy meat as the fires began licking at the hung beef and pork. Beer was being dispensed by white-clad, colored men, brought over from town for the job.

People strolled about, staring up at the still damp breast of the dam, at the rusting wheelbarrows and tools. But it was getting hot, and many sought the shade, to wait for the ceremonies.

Finally a handsome equipage crossed the low river, and under the fringed top sat Luther Sherrall and Senator Madison Baggett. As they alighted in the camp, they were immediately surrounded by a crowd. More and more vehicles rolled in, disgorging their human freight.

Hatfield waited until the crowd of perhaps three hundred men, women and children had collected in front of the speaker's stand. Through his glasses he watched the counsellor and Baggett climb the short ladder steps to the platform and take their seats at the center of a bench set for the speakers.

There were others on the bench. One was the moon-faced man whom Sherrall had introduced as Christian Vogel, heir to old Hans' lands. Bodyguards, men in white shirts and dark trousers, sat close to the counsellor.

The wagons had been driven back from the gathering, out of the way, and to give the horses shade. Most of the drivers had left the vehicles and joined the party. The gay murmur of voices was diminishing as Sherrall rose and made ready to speak.

The Ranger brought Goldy in through the woods and brush, left the sorrel as near camp

159

as possible, and went on, getting to the wagons by using them as a screen. His foes were concentrating on the crowds to whom they hoped to sell many thousands of dollars worth of stock and lots.

Near-by was a black buggy, with wide, curving sides which would hide the occupant except from directly in front. On the box dozed a white-headed old Negro man. Hatfield climbed in, and shook the driver awake.

'Pappy,' he said, and slipped a silver cartwheel into the Negro's hand. 'I got a lame foot, and I want yuh to drive me over to the party and let me sit there, on this side, just out from the crowd. See that flagpole? Take me there.'

'Yassuh, yassuh. I'll take yo'.'

'When we get there, I want you to go round mighty quiet-like and put this paper into Senator Baggett's hand. Yuh know him?'

'Yassuh, sho' do.'

'Don't give it to anybody else and don't let anybody stop you.'

The old fellow started his team of bony blacks and the buggy slowly rolled toward the crowd, the Ranger leaning back against the cushions. He could see from a diamond-shaped little peep-hole at the side of the black-leather top.

'Pappy' pulled up exactly as ordered. Counsellor Sherrall was speaking, waving his short, thick-muscled arms. His ugly face was red from the heat, and his bare head was matted with sweated hair. 'Now's the big moment,' thought the Ranger, hidden by the bulge of the buggy top.

'—and so, my dear friends,' Sherrall was saying, 'I decided to benefit our community and state by investing in this project, to irrigate the dry earth of the region by means of a mighty withholding dam.' The lawyer swept a hairy hand in a wide gesture toward the towering structure. 'The precious water stored through the rainy months will be held in the basin and distributed evenly to our customers.

'Our staff of scientists, chemists and soil experts, report that the land here will grow anything—grass and corn, any sort of crop you desire. Already many lucky people have taken advantage of this unparalleled opportunity to purchase sections and lots. If you do not wish to invest in a parcel of land at this time, stock in the water company may be obtained in limited quantities.'

The speaker paused to mop his brow with a silk kerchief. As he continued, Hatfield saw Pappy, the old colored driver, amble around the rear of the main stand. No one paid any attention to the bent old figure. Pappy looked harmless.

He paused behind Senator Baggett, and gently touched the politico's foot, looking up from where he stood and grinning at Baggett, saluting him. One of the bodyguards scowled

161

and started to fend Pappy off, but Baggett took the note and swung back to glance at it. Hatfield chuckled to himself as he saw the Senator jump and look nervously through the sea of upturned faces as though searching for someone.

'If he had any cute idea of crossin' me, that'll keep him on the track,' he thought.

'—and so, friends'—that was Sherrall going on—'I hope that you will enjoy every minute of our party here today. Eat hearty, drink hearty. Play around with your loved ones, for the world is bright and gay, and all is free for the asking. And now I will introduce to you the silver-tongued orator of the Pecos, that prince of speakers and great statesman whom you all know, Senator Madison Baggett!'

A roar of applause went up as the stout, beaming Senator came forward and bowed. Sherrall went back to his seat, to lean on his thick cane, to take a pinch of snuff.

Baggett's speech was the piece de resistance of the occasion. It was an era of high-falutin oratory and men with powerful voices and a capacity of flowery adjectives were always in demand. As soon as the Senator began it was apparent that he was a master at swaying crowds, much more of an expert than Sherrall.

He spread out his eloquent arms in an all-encompassing gesture.

'Today, my good friends, I am going to tell you the truth. Truth is a simple word, is it not?

Yet often it is difficult to determine. You are all fine, upstanding Americans. Texans, I know, or about to become citizens of our great State. There is no lovelier land on this green earth than Texas! My Texas!'

There was sugary emotion in Baggett's powerful voice. Tears started in his liquid eyes, and his hand went to his heart.

'No!' he bellowed. 'No other country, nor other state of our glorious Union can match the fair perfection of Texas. Across the broad sweeps of the mighty plains, the mountains and the rivers, the Border, the lush growths beside the Gulf where the broad Atlantic laves our sacred soil, the glory of Texas is rampant. What state can compare with her in size, in variety, in the myriad blessings of liberty and love and prosperity?

'Here we are part of that great commonwealth. Texans! We have a heritage of courage, of pioneer hearts which cannot be matched. Davey Crockett—Travis—Houston —Austin!'

He paused to allow the mounting cheers to die away.

'We have driven the savage Apache and Comanche from our soil. We have defeated the forces of mighty foes . . .'

As the Senator warmed up to his subject, the audience listened, spellbound, at his torrent of words.

'And here is Paradise! Those fortunate

163

enough to dwell on this fairest spot of the fairest of lands will be fed on milk and honey, blessed by the perfection of life which comes to few. Here, on the spot where I stand, will arise a mighty metropolis. Men will hurry to her, to quicken the arteries of trade. The cattleman will be here, with his vast wealth, the businessman will flourish, and the railroads will vie with one another to bring their steel lines to our very doors.

'Those who own this elected space on earth will find themselves millionaires overnight, by the sudden rise in value of their lands. They will travel, to Europe, to the Far East, to the Indies, in luxurious craft. They will be able to afford the equipages of kings, the homes of emperors.

'In this wonderful city they will find ultra-modern schools, hospitals, the greatest of physicians and scientists and one of the largest universities on earth—Paradise College. Paved streets, where men will be busy with the trade of the world, will bustle with activity, with the life-blood of commerce. Thousands of freight cars will enter and leave Paradise each twenty-four hours. Banks will overflow with the specie of our country. And this is what you are offered, dear friends—Utopia here, now!'

Baggett paused. His gestures were trained, designed to accentuate his speech.

A roar of applause, whistles, handclapping, went up. Hats were thrown in the air. Near the

Ranger, a youth was rolling on the ground, holding his sides as he laughed until tears filled his eyes.

'The old buzzard's outdoin' himself today,' the Ranger heard him choke out. 'He's hit the sky!'

The listeners were well aware that Baggett was exaggerating to the nth degree, but they enjoyed the flowery oration. It was a public sport to listen to such speakers.

The Senator faced them again. He was silent until they quieted. Then he raised both arms overhead and shook hands with himself, to the south, the west and the north.

Hatfield picked up the buggy reins. He had sent Pappy off to get a drink. Now Baggett had given the signal that Hatfield had ordered when they had spoken in Kent that night.

Baggett's mighty voice rolled clearly, distinctly, as he picked up again.

'Friends, I have spoken. Yet there is one important matter I must add.' He paused, and Hatfield knew that inwardly the Senator was quaking with fright, yet was actor enough to control it. As they waited to hear what he would say, Baggett shouted:

'The land here is good, the water will be forthcoming when the dam fills. But the control of that vital water will be in the hands of Luther Sherrall and a pack of rascals who are plotting to cheat you decent folks, to overcharge and bleed you by demanding

165

exorbitant rates! They have committed murder, they have dispossessed the honest ranchers of this vicinity, and bilked the workers of their money. Do not invest here unless they are arrested, and their ill-gotten gains taken from them!'

Luther Sherrall, unable to believe his ears as Baggett suddenly began to tell the brutal truth, leaped to his feet, started toward the stout Senator.

'You crazy old fool!' he screamed. 'Have you gone insane?'

CHAPTER TWENTY

THE GLORY OF TEXAS

Instantly, as Baggett saw Luther Sherrall coming at him with the cane, he ignominiously dived from the platform into the astounded spectators, with a howl of fright. Hatfield saw him crawling quickly under the stand.

The murmuring of the audience increased to a babbling, confused roar. Shocked at the turn of affairs, Sherrall sought to quiet them, hands raised, shouting at them.

The Ranger slapped the reins on the horses and sped around the outskirts of the crowd. And from the woods on the west, Bud Lockhart appeared running, at the head of a line of determined, armed men.

Hatfield came as close as he could to the stand, leaped from the buggy, and pushed through to the stairs, climbed up on the dais. In the bright light, the Ranger star shone on his breast.

'Texas Ranger!'

They saw his star, the tall build of the mighty officer, the sleek six-shooters in their pliant holsters, the determined but calm features. Luther Sherrall swung, his mouth gaping open as he recognized his arch-enemy, Jim Hatfield.

His bodyguards dared not draw. Before them surged the crowd, already buzzing angrily. A couple of Sherrall's hirelings quietly dropped off the back of the stand, hoping to save themselves by flight.

'Sit down, Sherrall!' ordered Hatfield.

A shot rang out on the hillside. Angry workers, cheated by the company, beaten by their guards, were pressing in, and the sentries, all paid fighters, melted away before them, running for the woods.

Sherrall was paralyzed for moments by the appalling situation. Baggett's betrayal had stunned him, and now the appearance of the Ranger, the flight of his aides, made him helpless. The moon-faced man who had posed as Vogel's heir had collapsed in his chair.

The counsellor hesitated, as the Ranger repeated his order. Then slowly he went to his seat. He had one hope left—Enrique Pereda.

Distant firing came from the east and north, in the direction of the Dot O. Hatfield and Baggett, who still was skulking under the platform from the wrath of his chief, were aware of what it was. The Senator, acting under the Ranger's orders, had sent a carefully timed message to Pereda, in Sherrall's name, telling him to hurry back to the camp.

Now Lockhart had arrived with his armed crew of tough laborers whose hate of Sherrall shone in their burning eyes. The crowd milled about, waiting for what the Ranger would do. Then their attention was drawn to the riders who splashed through the narrow stream up on the west bank. Enrique Pereda led a group of swiftly riding men and strung out behind them shooting back wildly at the pursuing Dot O, came the large band of gunnies, regulars and new men hired for the job.

Unaware of what had happened, Pereda was answering the call of his chief, Counsellor Sherrall. The Mexican knifeman turned his sweated black to the stand, ignoring a knot of spectators in his path.

'Here I am, Counsellor!' he shouted. 'What ees—'

He saw the tall Ranger then, and pulled his horse to a sliding stop. He threw up his Colt, firing quickly at Hatfield.

A Ranger gun replied. A dozen workers who hated Pereda even more than they did

Sherrall, let loose. Pereda was riddled. His horse, hit, rushed off, and the Mexican was spilled to earth.

His men saw him go down. They saw the Ranger facing them, saw the determined workers under Lockhart running to check them. And behind them rushed the Dot O, Oden and his ranchers, whooping it up in triumph.

The renegades turned, riding swiftly to the south, hunting a way out. Gunshots banged after them. Hirelings, and seeing that the game was lost, they sought only escape. Some were swept up in the trap, surrendering to the cowboys who pursued them.

As the Ranger gained full control, he signaled Lockhart and Oden to the stand. The rout of Pereda's large gang had sealed Sherrall's fate.

The crowd, burning with curiosity, quieted down at Hatfield's raised hands.

'Folks,' he said, 'Terence Oden will speak to yuh, and so will Bud Lockhart. They'll tell yuh what happened here.'

Oden spoke first. His powerful voice briefly described Sherrall's crimes. Lockhart took the stand next. He told of his part, and how Sherrall had shot down old Hans Vogel.

Baggett, realizing that Sherrall was helpless, emerged from under the stand and climbed up, to stand as close as he could to the Ranger. Among the crowd now were the workers, and many of Oden's friends. As the evidence mounted against the counsellor and his crew, angry murmurs grew to roars of rage.

The listeners began moving restlessly. Sherrall, frozen in his chair, turned white. He understood the threat.

'Lynch 'em!' shrieked a big fellow in front of the crowd. 'Lynch Sherrall and Baggett and the whole dirty gang!'

'Lynch! Lynch 'em!'

The crowd had become an infuriated mob, and lariats were quickly obtained. Ringleaders were surging toward the platform.

'Don't let them hang me; Ranger!' whined Baggett. His hand shook violently as he clung to Hatfield's arm.

The Ranger pushed the man behind him. He moved to the center of the stand, one man facing a multitude of angry people.

He indicated the Ranger star. His aspect made them quiet down to hear his words.

'I'm here, folks, to see that the law is carried out. Sherrall, Baggett and the rest are my prisoners. The Texas Rangers guarantee the lives and rights of all the State's citizens, no matter where they may be. The workers who built the dam will be paid.

'The dam will now be used properly. The water from it will be sold at cost, by common control. It won't be like what the Senator told yuh, but there'll be water to tide land owners over through dry spells, and it'll be a mighty nice spot to live in.

'There won't be any lynchin' bee. The Rangers don't go in for that. I'll protect my prisoners with my own life. Lynchin' is outlaw work, just what we are fightin' against. Counsellor Sherrall killed Hans Vogel and he'll pay for it, jist as the others will answer for what they've done.'

Terence Oden and Bud Lockhart stepped up, to stand one at either side of the big Ranger, showing they were with him.

'Three cheers for the Texas Rangers!' a gruff voice rang out from the crowd.

Everybody began yelling for the Rangers, for Hatfield, for Oden and Lockhart. It stopped the mob threat, and Hatfield started herding his prisoners down the steps, to get them out of the way. The crowd, good-natured again, headed for the food and beer.

Luther Sherrall leaned heavily on his stick. The Ranger was giving his personal attention to the Counsellor.

'Where to, Ranger?' asked Sherrall gruffly.

'I'll take yuh to Kent and lodge yuh in the calaboose there, Sherrall. Yuh'll be held for killin' Vogel.'

He wished to run Sherrall out of sight, before there was any more trouble. A horse was brought up. Goldy, answering the Ranger's shrill whistling, galloped in from the woods.

Hatfield ordered Sherrall to mount, and the

Counsellor put a foot in the stirrup. As the Ranger swung to leap on Goldy, Sherrall's face turned livid.

'This is all your doing, Hatfield!' he shrieked in hate and fear.

The thick cane rose, pointing at the Ranger. Sherrall sought to pull the trigger of the hidden gun inside the cane.

Hatfield had to shoot, a blinding, swift draw and fire, point-blank at the Counsellor. He heard the whirr of the .50 caliber slug sent from the cane-gun, and then Sherrall fell, his evil brain pierced by Ranger lead. One foot was caught in the metal stirrup as the startled mustang reared.

*   *   *

'Nice job, Hatfield!' complimented Captain McDowell. 'Them complaints that got sent in because Baggett, Sherrall and that trick of theirs might have harmed the Rangers' name but for yore quick thinkin' . . . Lockhart's all right, then, yuh say, and he's stayin' to see to the finishin' of the irrigation works.'

'Yessuh, and to marry Lily Oden, Cap'n. Sherrall's dead, and so's Pereda. Cheyenne Driscoll and Baggett, with a bunch we picked up, are bein' held for trial at Kent. The Vogel land, with the dam on it, has been bought in by Oden's bunch, and the water will be used right, for the good of all concerned. That hombre

172

that Sherrall set up as Hans' nephew confessed he was a liar and thief, and that the notes he had were forged ones.'

'There's a man's work to be done in Texas'—McDowell nodded—'and you shore fill the bill!'

There was always a call, somewhere, for the Rangers, in the vast reaches of the Lone Star State. Later, McDowell watched as Hatfield and Goldy moved off from Austin Headquarters once more.

'He carries the glory of the Texas Rangers with him,' muttered old Captain Bill.

We hope you have enjoyed this Large Print book. Other Chivers Press or G.K. Hall & Co. Large Print books are available at your library or directly from the publishers.

For more information about current and forthcoming titles, please call or write, without obligation, to:

Chivers Press Limited
Windsor Bridge Road
Bath BA2 3AX
England
Tel. (01225) 335336

OR

G.K. Hall & Co.
295 Kennedy Memorial Drive
Waterville
Maine 04901
USA

All our Large Print titles are designed for easy reading, and all our books are made to last.